Always Yours

by

Robin Jansen

Always Yours

Cover Art by *Jennifer Greeff*

The Wild Rose Press, Inc.
PO Box 708
Adams Basin, NY 14410-0708
Visit us at www.thewildrosepress.com

Publishing History
First Edition, 2023
Trade Paperback ISBN 978-1-5092-4635-9
Digital ISBN 978-1-5092-4634-2

Published in the United States of America

Slowly her eyes opened. A bright orb hovered overhead. After she acknowledged it with a shiver, it circled the room, gaining energy, and casting long shadows on the walls, as flickering rainbows shot out from the vanity mirror. Jemma's heartbeat picked up as chills pricked along her arms and down her back. Peeking over her covers, she remembered her therapist's words. "There's no such things as ghosts. There are no such things as ghosts. I'm asleep." Her voice sounded gravelly. She tightly shut her eyes, hoping the dream would change, deciding to focus on the man she met in her shop. But her mind was fuzzy, making it impossible to conjure up Benjamin's face or recall his voice. After several minutes, she slowly peeked out from the covers. Now the orb circled the bed, adjusting its speed slowly, as if observing her demeanor.

If this was real, Jemma mused, most people had relatives who arrived by plane or train, in cars, perhaps even by foot or Uber, but hers arrived not only dead but also in dead of night by way of her bedroom second-story window.

Praise for Robin Jansen

Dedication

Dedicated to Steven H. who encourages me and reminds me of the joy and happiness each day brings.

Many thanks to my editor, Jacki Hayes

Chapter 1

If pictures could talk, the fascinating stories they'd tell. The Little Shoppe of Ice Cream Delights held rows and rows of pictures, a kind of documentary cataloging the shop's earliest days on Mermaid Island. Jemma Singleton, the present owner, made sure the structure remained authentic to her family's original establishment, dating back to Great-Great-Great-Grandfather Harold Singleton. This place was her inheritance from her parents, as it had been from her mother's parents, and back and back for a myriad of generations. For that, she carried the responsibility of success on her nerves.

Jemma hummed as she lovingly straightened the crocked picture frames on the wall. The staid faces of her ancestors solemnly stared back at her from behind glass, and again she promised them she'd do her best to keep their dreams alive and added, "Even though you're all dead."

Jemma patted the recent email in her pocket. There was just enough time to read the printed copy one more time.

Dear, dear Jemma,
It was nice receiving your third letter this month, today, and learning more about the unusual place that you call home, in a family home built in the late 1800s.

Hearing it from you makes it all come so alive, something that reading online facts misses. I've often wondered how island living differs from the mainland. You helped clear that up. However, I can't help but wonder, have you ever dreamed of creating something else for yourself in another part of the world? What are the wild sexual dreams of an island shop girl? Tell me more. I am intrigued by your life.

Appreciating our correspondence,

Larisa Stewart, Author.

Ps. I am happily puzzled that you correspond by old-fashioned post office mail instead by the press of a button email, as I do. It creates a curious mystery which surrounds you and your life. Jemma, dear, your uniqueness stands out from my other fans. Refreshing! I'm positive that's what drew me to you, and why I personally respond to your pink enveloped letters, whenever I have time. They are precious as so are you.

And right then, Jemma felt puzzled over the usage of the word "nice" in Larisa's opening sentence. Surely, Larisa had an arsenal of inspiring words in her repertoire to choose. "Nice" was so vanilla. Oh well, she pushed away her small concern since Larisa also referred to her as "precious."

The fact that a popular romance writer had taken a special interest in her, forty-two-year-old Jemma Louise Singleton, made her positively giddy. Trying to still take it all in made her head spin. The author's fan club alone had to be close to one million members, but a simple ice cream shop keeper extraordinaire was the one who received personal attention. Of course, Jemma had to be careful not to let the secret out, in case the frugal businesswoman that she portrayed was laughed off the island. All day, Jemma would write and rewrite her response inside her head as she served her flavorful ice cream.

Bright daylight ribboned through the plate glass window, and the sea's tranquil movements were in stark contrast to Jemma's sudden rush getting ready for the day. She busily stacked the freshly washed and hand dried glass cups on the old marble countertop. The room smelled of slightly soured milk, sweet cream, vanilla, and baking waffle cones. To the customers' delight, she dressed in cream-colored uniforms, the same style as opening day, dating back to the 1920s.

The only deviation was the shoes: flat and pink with rubber soles, double knotted for safety reasons. It was a recent addition after receiving the delivery of the Larisa Stewart's novel *Where Romance Finds You* a year ago. For fear of societal ridicule, Jemma tried to temporarily hide it inside the walk-in freezer until the end of business hours when she'd carry it home to devour in bed. However, she slipped while placing the book behind a drum of ice cream. The injury resulted in a soft tissue damage which took weeks to heal, not to mention the temporary loss of access to the paperback. It was serendipitous because Derek was hired the day before the injury. Jemma put him in charge of the shop as she sat in the back office on a heating pad, writing letters to the romance author.

Not only did Jemma gush about Larisa's novels, but she also became emboldened enough to request the author write another tale about someone who never finds love but is just as happy single. Imagine her surprise when Ms. Stewart responded to thank her for the suggestion, which started a pen pal writing frenzy between them; well, almost a frenzy. Jemma wrote three letters to each one that she received. That was a year ago. Jemma kept score on her wall calendar. Larisa twelve. Jemma thirty-six.

Another glance at her wristwatch indicated her employee Derek was late, again. But the usual Monday customers, Pat and Beth Jenkins, were not. The elderly couple shuffled through the door, which rang the coiled spring bell above the door.

"You've saved our table by the window," the eighty-year-old man said, while holding the iron chair for his wife.

"It's permanently reserved for you, every Monday for the past twenty years."

Jemma kept track of how many visits her regulars made, noted on her calendar, to be celebrated with extra coupons for free ice cream. "Let's see. That makes about, one thousand twenty visits. Ya know, I should name this table after you two lovebirds," she jested. "You've earned it with all the hours you logged in over the years."

"Think of all those calories we've eaten," Pat mused rubbing his extended belly.

Jemma placed her hands on her hips. "Is it your special again? Or perhaps you are in the mood for something else, such as one of my newly created creamy flavors? I'd be delighted to list them."

"Nope. No new flavor for us," the couple agreed.

"The Mermaid Special, it is!" She snapped her fingers above her head.

"And if you are serious about naming the table after us, how about 'Love is in the Air, Table for Two'! In honor of my precious bride," Pat suggested. Beth reached across the table to squeeze his hand.

"Married over fifty years." Beth happily sighed.

"Congratulations on such a long and happy marriage. I'll get to work on that table name. It just needs a bit of tweaking. Don't want to make a hasty decision on such an important symbol of commitment." Jemma pinched the air with a twist of the wrist. At the counter, she filled the mermaid-shaped glass dessert bowl with jellybean vanilla, chocolate cranberry, delectable diva, and flamingo strawberry, placing one scoop next to the other all the way to the pectoral fins. Adding fresh fruit from her private orchard, Jemma dropped heaping soup spoons of fresh whipped cream on top. The finishing touch were two cherries.

"Don't forget the cherries," Beth called.

"Beth, have more confidence in me," she entreated, carrying the dish high above her head while singing a love song and dancing a two-step. She set her masterpiece in the center of the table with a long-handled spoon on a paper napkin at each place. "Have I ever forgotten them?"

"Where's your beau today?" Pat asked, shoveling up the cherries along with the ice cream.

"'Beau'?" Jemma wrinkled her nose at the term. "I have a beau? If so, I know not of him. Tell me more. Is he rich? Does he ride a white horse? A motorcycle will not do for me."

"Stop teasing. You know who I mean. That young man who helps you out in here. Dan?"

"Oh, you mean Derek," she corrected sweetly, as she always did with Beth's failing memory. "He's not my 'beau.' The kid is barely out of college. I'm old enough to be his ahh-h, older sister? He doesn't just help me out either. He's paid help, and right now he's late."

On cue, Derek hustled in through the back of the shop, stuffing the hem of a striped apron into his waist band. "I know. I know what you are about to say. Sorry. I was job hunting."

"That's this fifth time this month. Surely, you'd find something by now. Meanwhile, you're late for your one and only job. Impress your present boss by getting the Jenkinses water and more napkins."

"Yes, ma'am." Derek saluted, then hustled to obey.

"You are so pretty and smart, Miss Jemma. Unquestionably there must be someone who makes your heart race," Beth continued the conversation, not noticing Derek's arrival.

"I'm sure there's a string of them lined up every night to take her out." Pat bit into his cherry and handed the second to his wife who eyed him adoringly.

Derek laughed hysterically as he delivered the extra napkins and water glasses with chattering ice cubes to the table.

"Actually, I do have a line of men asking me out, quite often," Jemma enunciated each word.

Derek again howled.

"Truth be known, I'm too busy running this parlor to even think about anything else but business. It takes up all my time." Jemma lifted an eyebrow and mouthed "stop it" to Derek.

"I've worked here for a year, and personally witnessed all poor potential lovers actually weep over the unrequited love of Jemma Singleton." Derek dramatically bowed at the waist as he wiped invisible tears off his cheeks.

"Make time for love, dear. After all, despite your

many qualities, you are no longer a fresh catch." Beth nodded.

"Fresh catch, hunh?" Jemma huffed over the insinuation of her age and momentarily frowned, forgetting her manners. Thinking better of it, she decided to give Beth a break since her recent diagnosis of dementia. "I'll have you know that I put myself on ice, voluntarily."

"No worries. Jemma still finds plenty of time for romance. But sometimes it takes place inside the walk-in freezer." Derek pointed over his shoulder. "I know this."

"Oh my!" Beth's eyes widened. "I want to hear more."

"Really, Derek?" Clearly, her employee trampled her last nerve. "Pay no attention to the in-house idiot."

"Yep, there's gallons of ice cream flavors back there. All are her favorite, but she fell for only one of them. Yep, she fell hard. Right onto the cement floor. Sprawled out like an eagle. She can't hide her secrets like she thinks she can."

"You are quite the comedy act, Derek. Back to work." Jemma nervously peeked over her shoulder toward the wall lined with family pictures.

"Okay. Okay." He shrugged. "But I think you should create an ice cream flavor called 'Larisa Stewart's Erotic Night of Passion.'"

Up to this moment she thought her secret was a secret. Obviously, she thought wrong because Derek saw more than she knew about. *How much did that guy know and when did he know it?*

"How about an ice cream named Secret Life of Derek Dewberry?" Jemma sparred.

"Larisa Stewart. Boy, can that woman ever write about romance." Beth swooned, then in between her mouthful of chocolate with cranberry ice cream, added with sudden concern, "Of course, I've never read any of her books."

"Beth, you know about that woman's tawdry books?" Her husband furrowed his brow into a puzzled expression.

"I personally don't know, but I've overheard gossip. Jemma? Help me?" Beth called for backup.

"Can't help you, Beth. I've never read them either." Jemma focused her attention at the pictures and cringed when one of them rocked a bit, followed by another. *Please, please, not now.* "Pat, my question to you is how do you know about them?"

"Ah. I watch The Perch, the book review channel, every morning." Pat's eyes blinked. "But if Beth should ever want to read one of her books, I wouldn't object."

"Well, dear." She patted her husband's hand. "Then I might have one. Maybe two, lying around the house somewhere."

Pat kissed her cheek. "I'll help you look."

"Jemma always has a book in her hand," Derek said.

"Who's that man speaking?" Beth asked, perplexed.

"Derek. The man who works for me and isn't my beau," Jemma explained to Beth, then turned to Derek. "You know, I don't spend my time reading those type of silly books. I go for the more literary type, such as history of Mermaid Island, that is when there's even time to read."

Jemma oddly chuckled, then caught a glimpse of herself in the mirror that she usually avoided. Her focus shifted from romance back to reality. Forty-plus was more than a number. It was fighting rising cholesterol, turkey neck, the start of arthritis, lunch lady arms, and the facial lines of a middle-aged woman, a segment of the population largely ignored in literature, authors opting instead to write about young and skinny women with large perky breasts.

It reminded Jemma of her bosom, missing the perky part. She glanced down at her tight blouse to check out the button situation. They were ready to give way, so she had to avoid anything which required quick movement. Carefully, she sucked in, hoping it would make a difference. It didn't. Just this morning she ordered a size larger in panties. A set of matching ordinary beige, minus lace. A larger bra might be in her near future. Any type of lingerie would be wasted on this single gal, and yet she longed to be that type of gal.

The bell over the shop door rang. A handful of svelte women with open beach sarongs, revealing flat stomachs and tiny breasts, sauntered toward the counter. They ordered yogurt cups with fruit, then left without a glance at the owner. These invisible moments were common. Except for the island residents, she was treated as a non-person by tourists, whose only purpose was to serve them. Typical. No longer did that misled assumption bother her. They each had their own role to play. They consumed her product, and she took their money. Simple.

Watching them leave in such a carefree manner, Jemma's thoughts lingered on her youth, trying to recall how it felt to have infinite possibilities. A future wide open for choices, which she no longer had. Not that she was dissatisfied with her life. She wasn't. Since a young girl, she knew her eventual destiny would be right here, serving the islanders the best-made ice cream. Added to this pleasure, was her own self-created dairy creations. This year alone, she was personally responsible for a half dozen new delights which she named Fresh Blueberry Delish, Exploding Spangled Stars, Twilight on Blue Water, Love is a Beachy Affair, Anonymous, Always Yours, and Peach on the Beach.

Iron chairs scraped against the floor as Pat rose from his chair and helped Beth from hers. They both waved goodbye as they headed toward the door. At the last moment, Pat turned around as though remembering a forgotten thought. "Still the best ice cream in town."

"You mean, the only ice cream in town unless you buy it from the grocer," Jemma proudly stated.

"Hopefully so. That first shop on the boardwalk has a For Sale sign in the window the last two days. I hear it might already be sold and a new ice cream shop, catering to the young crowd with lots of noisy music, some arcade games, more options. That means competition for your place."

The picture of Great-Great-Great-Grandfather Harold pitched forward then slid off the wall, crashing to the floor. Jemma froze as Derek examined the frame and glass. "Hunh, not a scratch. I believe we have a summer miracle right here," he kidded. "It's our very own Christmas in July."

"True, that's nothing short of a miracle. Old glass is so delicate, it should've smashed into a thousand pieces," Beth said, watching it being rehung on the nail.

Jemma emotionally stumbled but quickly regrouped and walked the couple toward the door. "Thank you for your support all these many years and many more to come. I appreciate you both."

"We count on you for birthdays and holidays, and…" Beth looked around the room as though the thought she needed might be floating about.

"When our great grands come to town, too," Pat cut in and with a soothing manner, added, "Maybe it won't be another ice cream parlor. The rumors could be wrong. Who really knows what it'll be until it gets here?"

"A larger art gallery would be wonderful too," Beth suggested. "Pat, I could donate my watercolors to the place."

"That'd be nice but no time to talk." Pat squeezed his wife into his side. "I want to get Beth home so she can tell me more about those books. We might have an afternoon of reading ahead of us."

"Sounds like we are in for a good time." Beth giggled on their way out the door.

Jemma turned to Derek who quickly averted away from her stare. "I don't know where to begin. Should I start with the romance books, which is private information, or a new possible ice cream business on the boardwalk?"

"Your choice."

"Derek, you knew about the shop, didn't you? Why didn't you forewarn me?"

"I thought you already knew. Everyone else does. Besides, I didn't want to upset you. I know how flighty and dramatic you can be."

"Flighty?" Jemma tossed a wet rag at him. "I am not flighty. Maybe a tad dramatic but only when the occasion calls for it."

"Other than Tilly and me, there is no one in your life."

"So untrue. There's Fern and Alex and Amanda,

and…"

"I'm not talking about the other boardwalk shop keepers. I'm referring to real friends that you go to movies and lunch with. Who? Who other than me and those dead people on the wall, do you have?"

"Shush. They'll hear you." She looked over her shoulder at the pictures.

"Oh right. As if the pictures can actually hear you. You make up all this stuff to please the island's historical society. You can drop the charade with me."

She held her hands up and leaked an audible sigh. "Believe what you want."

"And every night, you shut yourself in here, going over receipts as though they are your only friend who might turn against you. I don't think you'd do well with competition."

"Changing subject: How did you find out about my romance books?"

"Who cares?"

Jemma leaned into the counter's freezer and scooped her newest flavor, Happy Almond Fudge, her go-to antidote to regain composure, along with happiness. That was all it took for the top button to give way with such force that it pinged against the opposite wall, then wobbled on its side, finally disappearing. *Where?* Jemma pushed aside chairs searching as the bell above the door tingled again.

"How may I help you?" She automatically asked. Straightening her back, she glanced up and saw him for the very first time.

Chapter 2

Just as the romance novels described, the ones she outwardly termed as foolish to everyone but secretly enjoyed when the winter wind brought inches of pelting ice and debilitating cold onto the island; there he stood: tall, dark, and handsome. Well, perhaps, if truth be told, he was minus a few inches to be actually termed as tall, which rendered him about her height at five foot seven, maybe eight. There protruded a bit of normal middle-age belly, with pants secured by suspenders. His face, so handsome it knocked your socks off at first glance. The perfect expression plated warm brown eyes and a huge smile. Dark curly hair swirled around his square face. If she didn't know better, she'd think he walked straight out of Larisa Stewart's novel, *When Love Finds You* Volume 1. The dashing hero's name? Benjamin Chandler.

This remarkable man stood only feet away, unaccompanied. No ring on his finger so therefore, unclaimed. The world faded. Only he remained. It felt like something from an old movie, but at present Jemma couldn't recall the title, nor who starred in it. Right now, she'd be lucky to recall her name, if asked. Jemma opened her mouth but couldn't speak. She lost all feeling in her throat. Words vanished. Somewhere, aloft, someone sang about love; although, she was sure it was Derek singing into his invisible microphone while leaning on the corner jukebox.

In that moment, she vowed never again to be embarrassed of romance novels. In fact, she'd be their advocate and confess to all that she was a romance novel junkie. Finally realizing, for the first time, those books were harbingers of good fortune. If there was such a thing of love at first sight, this was it. And tonight, she'd write Larisa Stewart to tell her all about this chance meeting, certain it'd be good fodder for her next book. Ordinary people could fall in love as well and books written about them be just as popular.

The man spoke. Sounds came from between his lips, but the words weren't clear, probably because blood rushed through her ears like a tsunami coming onshore. Her world came undone along with an errant piece of red hair that loosened from her tight bun and fell across her face.

"Huh?" was all she could manage which sounded more like a groan than an actual word. And just like that, she silently cursed every spoon of ice cream and dairy delight she ever consumed, yearning to be instantly reincarnated into one of those willowy beach women.

"Close your mouth. He only asked for one scoop of your most popular flavor, not those two vanilla-flavored scoops popping out of the double waffle cone you've strapped on beneath your clothes." Derek whispered into her ear. "And you might be a wee more alluring if you got rid of that chocolate mustache. It does nothing for you."

Snatching a paper napkin, she scrubbed around her mouth. Willing her brain to stop spinning in circles so she could think, and therefore speak, she searched her brain to remember which flavor was the best among all the flavors. And just like that, her voice returned. "I refer to it as Peach on the Beach. It's my own creation. There's bites of homegrown peaches in every scoop, along with candied sugar and tiny bites of crystalized ice, just like the olden ice cream."

"That'll be grand." The man intently perused the many ice cream flavors. "So, you also offer your home-grown fruit to the mix?"

"I do." Dang. Her affirmation to his question sounded like a wedding vow. She needed more words to offset the damage she may have incurred. "I also grow vegetables. Organic. I am very serious about what I do."

"I can see that. Ah, I'll just skip the veggies and stick to fruit in my ice cream. Make it that peachy beachy ice cream."

"Peach on the Beach." After rolling three scoops into a takeaway cup, she added more sliced peaches. Overfilled it with the juicy, wet, glimmering peaches then set it on the old marble countertop and watched the handsome customer reach for it. His fingers were slender and nail beds perfectly manicured. No wedding ring was noted. "Would you rather have it in a waffle cone? They are good too. No extra charge."

"No. This is just fine." His hand slowly slid into his pocket as he pulled out a ten-dollar bill. "Keep the change, Kid. Buy yourself something nice." He grinned, then met her gaze with a wink. As he turned to leave, something seemed to draw his attention downward. He paused. Eyes focused on the floor. The man bent. Picked up a small round object. "Someone lost something." He held her button in his open hand.

Oh dear, she had forgotten about that, and with a gasp, she looked down at her chest. There was her cleavage, four inches of it in plain view, but she couldn't really be sure without checking it out with a ruler. And her boobs did look like big ice cream globs of vanilla. For once, Derek was right.

If truth be known, relief swept over her remembering she wore her full-figured white bra today. It gave coverage but perhaps not enough. She hunched her shoulders forward with humiliation, hoping to make the double Ds less noticeable.

"No, no idea who the button belongs to. Certainly not me. All my buttons present and accounted for. It must belong to someone else. There were other people here earlier. Lots of people. Okay. Maybe not lots, but enough to have dropped that."

"How many customers does it take to pop a button?" Derek whispered in her ear.

"Those are a lot of words for a little explanation. I think I'll just leave the button right here on the counter. In case the owner returns for it." He set it on the counter, then slowly pushed the button across the space between them and left it on her side of the counter's edge. He stared at her bosom until Derek cleared his throat.

That's when the handsome man turned and slowly walked toward the door. *Goodbye, Benjamin.* The gradual frequency of his steps indicated he wasn't in a hurry to leave the shop. Jemma and Derek stood spellbound at his form until he jerked open the door and stepped onto the boardwalk. An errant wind shut it on his heels. Even the bell above the door rang sadly to see him leave.

"Wow." Jemma spun around and hurried to the plate glass window to peer down the street, still holding the cold sticky scooper in her sticky fingers, against her sticky chest. In her mind, she added a post-script to Ms. Stewart's letter in her head.

Chapter 3

After her nightly tub soak of lavender bath salts, she began her nightly beauty regiment of oils and creams. She rubbed them into her face, down her neck, over her body, extending to her limbs, making her skin butter smooth. Then in her pink cotton nightgown, Jemma quietly stepped out into the warm night air to get comfortable in her usual romantic spot where she'd write her correspondence. Settled into the squeaky porch swing, piled with fat pillows, a cool breeze found its way through her hair, lifting and twirling the red threads about her shoulders. The mood was set, sitting on the pillowed couch beneath the light of a half-moon. Stroking the pen onto paper made her quickly realize she couldn't read a single word of what she had written in the partial light of the moon. Jemma flicked on the yard light, opting out of the atmosphere in favor of seeing her words glide across the soft linen stationary. Tilly rested her head on her master's lap. Jemma stroked the cocker spaniel dog, then began the letter again.

Dear Larisa,
I hope it's okay I've called you by your first name these last few letters. We have been corresponding for a year now and thought it'd be okay to drop formalities. If I've taken too much familiarity let me know, and I will correct my brashness.

You asked several questions in your morning's email, which I quickly printed out and read. I hope to answer them in full and am relieved to hear you approve of my handwritten letters. Nowadays, people have lost, or not passed along, some of the personal touches of the past which I still find comforting.

Back to your questions. For ten years I attended culinary school where I focused on creating new flavors and desserts. Afterwards, I worked as a taste chef in a small New Orleans restaurant. Other than that, I've always lived on this island. I've traveled throughout half the country and found them all to have their own special beauty. However, Mermaid Island is my home and always will be from now on. When I came home from the mainland to take over my family business, I knew instantly this is where I belonged. The homestead sits on five acres and has been given modern updates throughout the years. I even built additional rooms to make it more comfortable, although I live alone with my dog, Tilly.

Many of my dreams have already come true. As you know, for the last several years, I've run a successful business, using most of the original ice cream recipes as I also comply with the ever-changing FDA rules. But I do have a dream or two, and time will tell if they will materialize. I think it's always important to have goals and dreams. How about you? Have you always wanted to be a writer? Your stories mean so much to me. They are filled with self-discovery, new beginnings, and love. But I do have another small suggestion. How about a heroine with a sweet and tender spirit, sporting a thick waist, and big out-of-control boobs, who finds love? And it wouldn't hurt if she had a mass of wild red hair. The hero and heroine should be portrayed as everyday people, because I am sure that's how your readers are, ordinary, like me.

Speaking of which, an engaging (isn't that an interesting word?) man walked into my shop today. He reminds me so much of your character Benjamin Chandler, not physically, but so venturesome acting. I probably made a fool of myself because the moment I saw him, it was love at first sight. Can that really happen? I know you write about it a lot, but is it possible in real life? Maybe it was his aura? Have you experienced love at first sight and did it last? I hope to run into him again. (FYI Here's a list of words that might be used in place of the word "nice." Lovely, fabulous, interesting, amazing, ducky, becoming, superior, engaging, curious, amusing, alluring.)

And you asked about my sex life. There's been no one. Not ever. Zip, nada. I refer to it as "Passover."

I've jabbered enough for one night. Looking forward to hearing from you. I hope you have love in your life. We all deserve to be swept off our feet.

Sincerely,
Jemma Singleton.

Carefully, she folded her letter into thirds, then slipped it into a pink already addressed and stamped envelope. Tomorrow morning she'd place it in her mailbox and put the metal flag up for the US Post Office mail woman. Jemma paused and looked at the feminine envelope. It might as well have the words CONFIDENTIAL INFORMATION written across it. To the eye, one would assume it was a love letter, all pink with her scrolly cursive letters. A tantalizing object to open and read, if one was so inclined.

Could the blabber mouth about her personal reading material be Loraine, the mailwoman, not Derek? She could be the leaky link in spreading her private secrets, especially when the books arrived. If so, that meant everyone on her route, and workplace, must know by now of her very private correspondence. That could be how Derek found out. Certainly, reading her letters would be against the Federal government rules, right? Wasn't there some sort of oath they had to take about privacy, or something? For now, she'd trust her friend and believe the best. It'd behoove her to keep an eye out just the same. The last thing she needed was for the post office to be like the island's beauty salon, rife with gossip. Maybe this was a good time to switch to email.

Jemma fell into bed, exhausted from the sparring thoughts revolving in her head. She needed her reputation to remain pure, her secrets kept, ice cream flowing, and customers returning. A mental break was needed in order to remain calm and focused. It was important she give full attention to new ice cream recipes. Again, that posed another problem because it required more room due to the fact the current shop was too small.

There wasn't room to do more than scoop and serve and seat a half-dozen crammed-together customers. Sure, there was a back room, but it was for hanging coats in winter, and hats in summer, next to the dozen or so aprons. Even the tiny office space was crowded with the computer and paper files. And the kitchen here was not laid out properly to shelve all the needed ingredients. She let out a full body sigh and rolled to her side, noticing she hadn't shut off the outside lights. Suddenly, she was too tired to do anything but close her eyes. Her mind slowed. A serene floating feeling encapsulated her body. In a dreamlike state, her mind numbed, as a giant wave rose.

Chapter 4

"Jemma. Excuse me, Jemma. You need to wake up now."

No. I'm swimming. Leave me here.

"Jemma, I need to speak to you."

Wind caught the sails of the Jemma's craft. A gush of water crashed over the sides, purging her ruminations. Although her nightclothes were soaked with salt water, she didn't move. At the moment she felt neither awake nor asleep. The realization of being home, in bed, grew.

Slowly her eyes opened. A bright orb hovered overhead. After she acknowledged it with a shiver, it circled the room, gaining energy, and casting long shadows on the walls, as flickering rainbows shot out from the vanity mirror. Jemma's heartbeat picked up as chills pricked along her arms and down her back. Peeking over her covers, she remembered her therapist's words. "There's no such things as ghosts. There are no such things as ghosts. I'm asleep." Her voice sounded gravelly.

She tightly shut her eyes, hoping the dream would change, deciding to focus on the man she met in her shop. But her mind was fuzzy, making it impossible to conjure up Benjamin's face, or recall his voice. After several minutes, she slowly peeked out from the covers. Now the orb circled the bed, adjusting its speed slowly, as if observing her demeanor.

If this was real, Jemma mused, most people had relatives who arrived by plane or train, in cars, perhaps even by foot or Uber, but hers arrived not only dead but also in dead of night by way of her bedroom second-story window. At last, the sphere settled on the foot of her bed and the weighty transforming figure caused the bed springs to sink in and squeak. Great-Great-Great Grandfather Harold appeared, suited in dress clothes as though he had come from an important party. His thick gray hair was neatly slicked back off his forehead. A handsome figure still, even in dissolution. It all seemed so real as her mind stuck between reality and fantasy.

"Jemma." When he said her name, she noted love in his voice which served as a release valve quieting her qualms.

"You've come alone this time." Real or imaginary, it was always good to see him again.

"There was not sufficient time to put the crew together. It seems I was the only one who was able to cancel a previous engagement."

Waking further, Jemma snickered. "What engagements do the dearly departed have?"

"You'd be surprised. There's still plenty to do and people to see. One day you will know for yourself." He fondly smiled.

"I'll wait. Not that I don't want to be with you, but I want to stay on this side of mortality for a bit longer." She yawned.

"It's not your time yet." His eyes were clear blue, like a calm sea. It was good to see him in color and not in the usual way; the black and white pictures made him appear remote and one dimensional.

"Will you come for me when it is?" The transition

between worlds would be difficult enough but so much better with a friend to guide her.

"No, not I. That's the job of your parents."

Without thinking, Jemma grabbed for Harold's hand but only grasped air. "How are they?" She swiped at her sudden tears. The heartache about their loss was still acute.

"They are grand. No worries. Stop weeping."

"Why don't they come for a visit like you and the others?" Her heart ached to see them once more. She'd give anything to hear their voices. Maybe her mother would remind her of the pie crust ingredients. No matter how hard Jemma tried, she couldn't recall how to get it so flaky. And her dad. He told the best stories of when he was a boy.

"It's not their turn. They haven't been gone long enough and are still adjusting. You are still adjusting as well, learning to be without them and stand on your own. That's why we all come from time to time, to help guide you."

"What's it like over there?" Jemma leaned forward with concern. "Boring? Sad? Horrid?"

"It's splendid! Learning still continues. Discoveries each day. No one is bored or idle. Now enough of them. We need to focus on the here and now. I have come about other matters that've been brought to my attention."

"Is it my stash of books or letters?" She braced for his temper, which flared easily.

"No, not at all. I can't be concerned over small details like what you read. Bah!" Smoke blew from his ears. That was a new one for her to observe. Relatives appeared on occasion for various reasons. Comfort was the primary reason whereas some were only concerned with the business end of the shop, while others enjoyed micromanaging her, ranging from the correct placement of silverware, to explaining how to properly fold napkins, the right way to count out change, to polite conversations. That was it. Harold had to be here because of today's conversations.

"You must agree that it's endearing the Jenkins want to name their table something romantic. I think it would be a quirky addition to the shop," Jemma teased, then placed her hands on her lap, trying to get ahead of the pending conversation.

"If the tourists enjoy it, then it's okay by me. In the meantime, girl, open your ears. Talk of a new ice cream shop on the island is afoot."

Jemma covered her mouth with a blanket to stifle the laughter due his old ways of speaking, that occasionally came out of her mouth as well.

"You need to be on top of this matter," he scolded gently.

"It may not even be another ice cream shop." Jemma tried to defend herself from not being more proactive on matters.

"I bet it is, and it's an off-islander who will own it. They're the ones with all the money. Trust me on this one. I am never wrong."

"I'll look into it later today." Jemma glanced at the 3 a.m. clock.

"Good." Harold leaned toward her, planting his hand firmly on the blankets. "Find out all the information you can. Who is the owner? Do they come from a good family? What dairy do they use? Who the manufacturer is? I have laid in your hands a great generational gift. Do not be sidelined with other matters. Understand?"

Jemma nodded. "I understand."

"Important matters are entrusted to you. See to them. Let nothing distract you."

"I hear you. I won't. First thing in the morning, I will check it all out."

A whine came from a shadowed corner of the room, as strings of colors spun as webs.

"What was that?" Jemma jumped in surprise.

"Oh, that's Latimer. He wanted to come along and meet you."

A small spirit wearing short pants, a white top, and brown leather shoes with dirty socks shyly stepped out.

"Come here, young lad. Meet your cousin four times removed, Jemma."

A shy five-year-old took big steps to her.

"Hello, Latimer. Nice to meet you."

"Take me on a trip," he timidly spoke.

"A trip?" Jemma asked, feeling confused.

"I want to ride in a car. Sit on a horse. I died from the Spanish flu. I want to see life here."

"Ah, so you had a reason to tag along after all, my young lad. Not an altruistic one of meeting your cousin. You see, Jemma, he's starting to create all sorts of havoc up there." Harold pointed out the window.

"And perhaps now he's ready to create some excitement for me." Jemma recoiled with the thought of trying to keep track of a little specter. Even dead, he could cause major chaos. Jemma turn her attention to the smallest spirit yet to visit. "Impossible, Latimer. You cannot stay with me on Earth. I have important matters that need sorting. Besides, this is my busiest season and I have my shop to tend to."

"I don't want to be in the shop. I want to take a trip

somewhere." Latimer bit his lip and moved toward the bed aggressively.

"Latimer, Jemma is right. Another time she will take you on a car trip. Now is a bad time." Harold's mood grew intense.

Latimer scowled. Removing the blue and red tin whistle from his pocket, he blew on it. A high-pitched squeal wheeled from the instrument making Tilly bark.

"Be off with you, Latimer," Harold shouted, causing the unlit ceiling fixture to wildly swing.

Latimer nodded, grew wings, and flew out the window.

"That was interesting." Jemma raised her brows.

"The child means well." Harold stood and collectedly moved away from the bed. "Sleep well, Jemma."

Jemma stared at him for a long moment, recalling his initial visit. It so unnerved her at the time, it sent her racing to a therapist's office. According to Sarah Buntfield, Jemma conjured her visits of dead relatives because of her need for family. However, with time, Jemma relaxed and started to revel in them, becoming increasingly reluctant to release the fictional visions.

They offered business advice, and she took it. Why not? It was proved to be solid, and she wasn't one to turn down good advice. The dearly departed aunts from generations past offered solace, which she often needed, especially at the time of her parents' death. They comforted her and made her feel less alone. And then there were the relatives who served no other purpose but to make her laugh and entertain her. Without a living relative left on earth, she gladly turned to the dead ones. Holidays and birthdays were the hardest. They were usually busy with their own new traditions on the other side. At such times, she pushed herself to go out more, even if it was alone. Enlarging her nonexistent circle of friends was challenging.

Jemma leaned back against her pillows. Doubt was sparring tonight with her senses, feeling herself once again teetering between reality and fantasy. What were those new mantras for a Happier You she recently downloaded? Jemma grabbed her phone off the nightstand. "My potential is limitless, and I choose where to send my energy. What I see is not always real. I need to stay connected to life and the living," she read. The promise of serenity failed to deliver a happier you. Jemma released her phone and promptly lost it in the bed covers. Expecting to find an empty room, she opened her eyes expecting to see Harold gone. But he wasn't. He was doing something for the very first time, silently sitting in the rocking chair, watching over her; his great-great-great granddaughter.

In that moment love engulfed her. She wasn't alone and knew if Harold had anything to do with it, she never would be.

She turned on her side and sleep came abruptly.

Chapter 5

The morning mist rolled across the bay area as shops gradually opened. For once, no customers, it was still quite early. Just as well since Jemma was again greeted with lopsided and upside-down family pictures. Starting at the front of the shop, she tipped each picture back into place until all twenty-five were in perfect order. The yard-long picture of the first and second generations of Mermaid Island's Singletons with their young children hung mid-center. Fanning out from it were individual portraits of Harold, his brothers, and sister. Then came the great-great-aunts and uncles, the great-uncles and aunts, the aunts and uncles and subsequent cousins. Jemma balked at the idea of adding her parents' faces to the wall due to the pain involved in that constant reminder. An added sense in having lost her anchors, the very spot in her heart the ancestors tried to fill with night visits. Jemma knew she survived by remembering she was loved. By now the hurt was so commonplace that it had softened until she hardly noticed it as a part of her.

What chilled her was the boy in the yard-long picture, Latimer, who no longer stood holding his mother's hand. Instead, his arms were crossed over his chest. The scornful expression on his face was hard to miss. It made her laugh at him. Odd how they could change expression in something so static as a photograph. Derek would be at the shop soon. How could she continue to explain her ghostly visits to him? For once, she'd say nothing to him about it. It was maddening always to see his skeptical expression no matter how many times she readjusted the frames.

Right now, she'd focus on the list of questions she was given by Harold to find the answers. Rarely did shops come up for sale. The last one was over ten years ago. The only way to stop a possible off-islander from buying the shop was for her to purchase it, which was a move Harold would definitely approve of her doing. She needed to act fast. Opening an additional ice cream shop of her own, making it a two-store chain, was possible. But should she be considering other possibilities? What else might she want to do with it? An art gallery for local artists, as Beth suggested? A small eatery? But that would put it in competition with her friends with similar shops. A second-hand shop? Filling up with gallons of questions, Jemma glanced out the window as the frolicking water beat up the soft sand. She tipped her head in deliberation as Derek walked in.

"Look at the long picture," she politely requested.

Derek stood in front of it. "Okay. What now?"

"Find the little boy near the center of the picture. What is he doing?"

"Such odd requests you make of me." Carefully he sorted through all the people and faces. At last, he answered, "There he is and he is holding his mother's hand. What a big grin he has too. Anything else I need to look for?"

"What? Are you sure?" Jemma quickly hurried to the wall to see for herself. "You're right. Holding his mom's hand, or who I presume is his mom, and smiling. That's just what he's doing."

"Was that a training in futility?" Derek sarcasm was at its peak.

Feeling deflated, Jemma shook her head.

"You have made me curious about him."

"His name is—was Latimer," she corrected herself. "He died from the Spanish flu. Never rode a pony. All I know."

"How'd you find that out?"

Quickly she changed the subject in case her sanity was called into question. "I noticed the new shop this morning when I pulled up."

"Impossible. Your parking spot is right out back. You can't see that place from there."

"All right. I deliberately looked. Good spot. Next to the parking lot to the beach."

"I hear a but."

"But we have a much better location." She faced Derek. "We are the first shop right on the beach and—"

"Where's all the customers today?" Derek cut in, looking around the empty room.

"Still in bed on this cloudy and chilly day, I imagine. Soon enough the day will warm, and when that happens, they'll arrive. You'd know that if you were on time more often." Jemma spun about and looked out the side window. "The problem with this place is, there is no place to expand and not much by the way of seating. Maybe I should make a patio on the side of the building and add tables and chairs. What do you think?"

"It's pretty breezy here with us directly across from the beach. Blowing sand just might be a problem. Peach on the Beach ice cream will work as a name, but Beach in Ice Cream might not be a popular selection to eat."

Jemma walked to the backroom and soon emerged

wearing casual clothes, holding a floppy hat. Her hair was bunched into a messy ponytail. "Since we are short on customers, I am going to sit in front of the shop for sale and watch traffic flow. Walk around the place, peek in the windows."

"That's not obvious," Derek chided.

"I don't want anyone to know my interest yet, so I am disguised as a tourist."

"And you think you are incognito? In just those capris and that tie-dyed shirt?" Derek rolled his eyes.

"Everyone wears shorts or capris or skimpy bathing suits on the island. I need to fit right in. And what's wrong with my tie-dyed shirt? Not one thing, I say. Note my flip flops, too, please." She held up her foot, sensible shoes be damned. She'd take her chances on tripping in them. "I'm part of the crowd today and will stroll about, unnoticed. Comparison shop especially if it's another ice cream shop as predicted. Know thine enemy."

"I think it's supposed to be 'know thyself."

"Not where I come from."

"You're from here."

"Details." Straightening the again-crooked, black-and-white. yard-length picture, she noted how the men stood as soldiers next to one another, while the women sat in front wearing summer white. And there was that stinker, Latimer, with his arms crossed and scowling, again. Just for her benefit, she supposed. She murmured, "Don't worry, I have this all under control."

"And I've got the shop under control."

Jemma slung on her hat, pulled out her ponytail in the back, put on her game face, and set off in the direction of the new competition. "It's go time. But first, it's my morning to see the therapist."

Jemma listened to the sounds of the seagulls arguing over beached shrimp, she took in the sights of shops in their early stages of opening for the day and watched as fishing boats buzzed out to sea. The warming sun felt good on her arms and face as she stepped onto the boardwalk. The nippy breeze off the water revitalized her spirit. For now, she was like everyone else, enjoying the privately owned colorful little shops, the salty sea air, and the invigorating bustle she usually only saw from the backside of plate glass windows. There was something to be said about taking a day off. Perhaps she'd do a bit of shopping. Oh, but wait, she was on a mission. That came first, right after her session.

"Morning, Jemma. Keep up the good work." Jonah, the president of the Historical Society, greeted her in passing. "By the way, I have heard rumors about the shop for sale down at the end of the boardwalk."

"Oh? And what are those rumors about?" Jemma feigned noninterest.

"I hear it might be a new ice cream shop. I hope I'm wrong. Especially for your sake."

"I hope you are as well and that an islander buys it. We need to keep our profits here."

"Couldn't agree with you more. I think we all need to do something about this," Jonah urged.

"Like what?"

"I have some ideas and will get back with you." Jonah disappeared down the boardwalk.

Perplexed over being recognized so quickly, Jemma momentarily remained in her tracks. How could she be recognized when out of uniform and not in context inside the ice cream shop? It'd be horrid if someone saw her checking out her possible investment. Smelling a good deal made people bolt to buy, or reassess their island needs, especially when it came to profiteering. Jemma reached into her purse for sunglasses. Setting them on her nose, she felt more confident as a tour bus pulled to a stop in front of her with a long loud hiss.

Only two steps further, she again heard her name. "Jemma?"

Fern from Fern's Restaurant came running. "I was just about to call your shop when I caught a glimpse of you in passing. I'm in a terrible situation. Just got a call from my mainland supplier, and his fresh lettuce crop was destroyed by slugs during the night."

Jemma set her hand on his arm to calm Fern. "No worries. Just this morning I pulled all my lettuce from the garden, and I have five bushels full: butter lettuce, spinach, romaine. What do you need?"

"I'll take it all." He wiped his brow with relief. "You saved me. Thank you."

"It's my pleasure. They're in the shade on the side porch. Pick them up and they are yours."

Fern gave her a full-on hug and kissed her forehead. "You're the best. Do you happen to have any berries? I need several gallons of your vanilla ice cream, too."

"If you pick the berries, you can have 'em. But you'll have to pay the going price for the ice cream."

"No problem."

Jemma caught another hug from Fern before he headed to his truck.

"Good morning, Jemma! Is this your day off?" Alex called from the surfboard shop. "How about a surfing lesson today? Amanda would love to teach you."

"Ah, not today. I am pretty busy and have another appointment and all. Thanks anyway." Jemma gritted her teeth and pulled the brim of the hat further down over her brow.

"Wait." Alex hurried to Jemma with a poster in his hand. "I know I am asking a lot but would you mind hanging this in your window? Advertising a surf sale."

"I'd be glad to." Jemma carefully rolled the sales poster up and stuck it into her large purse.

The dress shop window display caused Jemma to slow her step. The mannequin modeled a patterned dress of tropical green and orange flora, held up by spaghetti straps. Next to the mannequin's arched, impossibly small feet, were a pair of matching dainty sandals. "How clever. An ensemble."

Usually, at times like these, she'd come up with a new name for her latest ice cream creation on the spot, like Bird of Paradise Flair, or A Tropical Walk. This time, nothing came to mind. Maybe she'd take a minute, just one, to go inside and have a closer look at the dress material. And price. And size. Not that she planned to actually buy it.

The sales lady crept up quietly. "It's you, Jemma."

Jemma jumped. "Oh, geez, Audrey. I didn't hear you. You gave me a start. Whew. Give me a second to catch my breath. Okay, I was just passing and saw this dress. It's not for me, but for…" Her voice trailed.

"It'd look perfect on you. Let me see if I can find it in your size. Follow me."

"Oh, I really don't have the time," Jemma protested as she willingly followed along obediently as an excited puppy.

"Ah, here it is. I say, you probably take a size sixteen, am I right, dear?" Audrey held up the dress.

Jemma brightened, grateful a size eighteen hadn't

been suggested. "Yes. That might work."

Audrey removed apparel from the rack and took it into the dressing room along with shoes. "If these shoes are too small, let me know. I have more in the back."

Jemma stood alone in the dressing room, looking at herself in the full-length mirror. This was the last place she wanted to be, along with checking out her competition. If she had her way, she'd be smeared in sun tan lotion and lying under a big umbrella on the beach, reading Larisa's latest book. However, the dress hanging on the hook made her happy. Well, it would take only a minute to try it. She dropped her pants and stepped out of them. Flung her hat on the chair and removed all her clothes but left her underwear. She touched the dress and found the material to be breathable cotton with enough spandex to keep it from wrinkling, a very important clothing summer feature these days, especially when one's borders were a bit expanded. Slowly she tugged on the dress. It fit. Lord in heaven, she got herself into a new dress and breathed a sigh of relief because it fit. The gorgeous dress fit.

Audrey opened the dressing room door and asked, "May I help you in there?"

"It fits. It fits. It fits," Jemma sang out as she pushed the door wide and raised her arms in victory. "Ta-da! It fits!"

"Great. Now just let me zip you up."

"Zip me up? Oh, you mean it wasn't already zipped?" Jemma scowled as Audrey pulled and tucked, as the zipper slowly rode up.

"Do you have any shapewear at home? We have a fresh stock. Let me get you some."

"Wait. I may already have some at home." Jemma

frowned, deciding against the dress.

"Let's try on those shoes before we wrap it all up."

"Before we 'wrap it all up,' I need to think about it a bit more. There's errands I need to run."

"I understand."

Escaping from the clothing shop felt absolutely freeing. What was she thinking anyway? Duh. The dress, although really her, was for one thing too tight, and for another, there wasn't any place to wear it. And those ridiculous shoes. Her feet, which were by the way a size 9 wide, would stick out either side, most likely causing her to fall and sending her to the hospital. Then what would become of her shop? Have Derek run it? She let out a short but hearty laugh. No way.

Jemma plodded onward, feeling confident in her disguise again, until the tip of her right flip flop caught in the unexpected gap in the walkway, causing her to stumble into a tattooed tourist. He said, "Dude, careful. You are such a klutz."

Perhaps someone needed to remove her from the detective game before someone got hurt. Namely herself. But she'd never be able to explain it to her picture people. A handful of yards later, she arrived at her destination. There, to her dismay, a new sign leaned against the building. *Mermaid Island's Best Ice Cream Shop.*

Anger, as she had never allowed herself to feel up to this moment, exploded inside her body. Jemma's cheeks burned with furor.

"Looks like an off-islander bought the place already," an island resident sadly noted.

First dibs needed to go to someone who lived year-round on the island, not a summer intruder from the mainland. Something very close to wrath simmered just below the surface, fueling her. Not knowing how to properly process her feelings, she was thankful to be on her way to visit Sara Buntfield, who wasn't just the best therapist on the island but also the only therapist on the island.

Chapter 6

Sara's office was done in soothing tones of greens, blues, and grays, a tribute to the colors of the sea. Most likely it put people into a relaxing mood in order to freely express thoughts and feelings, instead of disguising their emotions. Jemma sat in her usual seat, which faced the ocean and figuratively rode the waves out into the ocean where she lived in perfect serenity. She settled her arms on each armrest, leaned back, and felt the cushiony fabric press into her back. If any time warranted a mantra, this was it. "I am one with the sea," she breathed.

"How's it going?" Sara sat with one leg crossed over the other.

"Good." Jemma slid one hand down her pant thigh and opened her eyes, surprised Sara had snuck into the room so quietly.

The therapist was Jemma's age but, unlike Jemma, made weekly visits to the beauty salon and nail salon, where true to her confidentiality agreements, she never uttered a syllable about her clients, no matter how much the others pressed. Her business boomed as a result, for gossip ran rampant as summer tourists in the small community. Her intellectual health was reflected by her healthy frame. Sara was dressed in tight fitting clothes, which were feminine and revealing. They looked wholly uncomfortable to Jemma.

"How's your stress levels?"

"A bit high, but I'm in the mid-calming-myself phase of the morning." She glanced at the eleven o'clock time and corrected, "Late morning."

"What do you think is the source of your stress?"

Jemma didn't move, nor did she answer. She was fully immersed in sailing out to sea.

For once, she didn't want to discuss her relatives. Today she felt the need to protect them, figments of her imagination or not, especially since Harold had sat most of the night with her. Imagination or not. For just today, she needed safe harbor from storms. If Sara removed that, she might be swept off to sea.

"Anything special you want to discuss?" Sara didn't press. She was a patient one.

"I'm really angry right now."

"What are you angry about?" Sara leaned forward. "Take your time. Gather your thoughts."

"No need for thought gathering. An old established shop on the boardwalk must have been bought already because there is a sign left out in front of it. In the shape of a mermaid, which is my signature ice cream dish. Mermaid Island's Best Ice Cream Shoppe, it reads. How can they say that? Was there a vote on it somewhere that I don't know about? A poll taken? I think not." Jemma crossed her arms and concentrated on the waves. Her chest hurt. Perhaps she was about to have a heart attack.

"Why does that upset you?"

"It's a snub to me. Not respectful. Plus, they could take a large percentage of my business away." Jemma now focused her sight on Sara waiting for her to look just as upset. After all Sara was an islander too. Every business was in this together.

"Valid points. Let's play worst case scenario. Just suppose that's true. And let's suppose that it does hurt your business. Do you feel you are losing control of something?" Sara wasn't smiling.

Jemma narrowed her eyes. Did Sara's expression mean she knew something about the shop Jemma didn't know? And why was there a sudden whoosh of the ocean sounding in her ears? Had she gone overboard emotionally?

"I'm losing control of my future. My past is gone. The shop's future is all that's left."

"It scares you."

"It makes me furious."

"You need to learn to control the angry impulses you have." Sara leaned forward in her chair.

"I can't sit back and just wait. I need to take immediate action." She hit the armchair with her fist.

"Are these dangerous thoughts you are having?"

"What I want is to throw the freaking sign into the ocean. But I won't," Jemma reassured her. "I feel as though I am losing control over my life since my livelihood is being threatened."

"You have lived off the island, went onto further education."

"Culinary. I went to culinary school."

"Yes, and then you were hired at a job you enjoyed for many years. You have been successful in the past and continue to be. Those successes will carry you into the future. You have talents. Your life isn't just tied into this island."

Wanna bet? How could I leave my home and my ancestors? What would Harold and Vera and Latimer and all the rest do without me? Jemma pictured herself sitting in a dinghy being carried by waves into the unknown as dark clouds loomed above.

"I was happy in that job until my parents passed. Life changed for me drastically. I ran home to this island.

I feel I'm embraced here. It's my forever home, and I can't lose it. Here, I am whole. I'll never leave to live someplace else. My roots grow in this sand. It's important I find out who bought the shop, and if another ice cream place is going in, I need to find out who it is, who their distributor is, what their plans are. I must fight for what is mine."

"You've had another visit? It's obvious." It came as a statement rather than a question. Sara appeared to scrutinize Jemma.

"Don't blame this on my family," Jemma whispered. A far-off whistle blew. Latimer?

"But the root of your fears is based on your need to invent people. Dead people."

"That's beside the point. One hasn't anything to do with the other. In my mind there is no connection."

"Let me guess. It was Harold who appeared. And he was concerned over the business."

"Yes," ashamedly she answered. And now Sara would go off point and blame it all on her need for family, instead of the reality of the new shop. At least she didn't know about the newest ghost's appearance. He'd remain safe from Sara's scrutiny if she kept him a secret.

"Just now, when you told me your concerns over the new shop, you were echoing his exact words. Am I right?"

"In a way. More like his sentiment."

"Jemma, let me be blunt. They are your words. You are projecting them onto him, someone who you feel is smarter and more capable. But you are capable. And smart. You can figure this out without this imaginary cast of characters."

"It sounds as though I haven't confidence in myself."

"I didn't say that. We are trying to get to the root of your visions so you can move forward with your life. Jemma, these visits are only nightmares, a mirror of your insecurities. They aren't real."

"But they feel real. I didn't know what the questions were to ask until Harold told me. Doesn't that prove that I am actually visited by my family spirits?"

"People have a deep faith in the afterlife. But I have yet to hear anyone express regular visits from anyone who continually crosses over for chats."

"I feel more confused than ever." Jemma found herself mentally deserted on a sandbar.

"Oh dear. We seem to be regressing." Sara shook her head with downcast eyes. Now Sara was the one looking out to sea. Being a people pleaser, it was hard to see Sara's disappointment. "Jemma, you fantasize when you feel afraid, or lonely, or sad."

"Confused too. Don't forget confused." Jemma crossed her legs and jiggled her foot. Feeling very defensive probably will bring on another visit, which Sara would refer to as an "episode."

"I see our time is up. I'm so sorry. I think it's important we talk again soon." She pulled out her appointment book. "How about tomorrow, same time?"

"I need to check my calendar. I'll get back to you." Jemma stood and adjusted her tight capris at the waist, then shot out of the office. The sun was quite high by now, and the glare off the shop windows was piercing. The nearby bench was the place to sit and steady herself to catch her breath. Fishing through her purse to find her sunglasses, she saw him. Benjamin Chandler. Not his real name but close enough. She'd never forget the first words he spoke to her. "I want your bestselling ice cream." Here he came, walking directly toward her, then around her, and now past her.

"Hello?" She waved. Between the shop being sold, the frustrating therapy session, then being fully ignored by a possible love match, it was just too much. She stood and stamped her foot, creating a reverberation in the boardwalk. "Excuse me."

He turned and blinked. "I'm sorry. Did you say something?"

"Indeed, I did. It was 'hello.'" She offered a quick wave as her throat turned desert dry. She needed water to quench her thirst from talking so much during the last hour but managed to smile and eke out, "I'm Jemma, shop proprietor extraordinaire. Not this one with the braggy sign. I have the shop way, all the way down the boardwalk, right on the beach. The Little Shoppe of Ice Cream Delights."

He appeared perplexed.

She wiggled her fingers in the correct direction of what she meant before removing her hat and sunglasses to insure he'd have a better look at her face. Everyone else seemed to recognize her. How come not him? Evidently, she was the most forgettable gal on the entire island. That explained a lot, never having dated in the last fifteen years, except that one time when she thought the fishing harbor boat captain at the wharf asked for a date, when he only meant to sell her the fresh fish of the day. From that day to this, she avoided that section of the bay. It was a most embarrassing moment of her entire life, only to be outdone by today's fiasco.

"Does the name Peach on the Beach mean anything

to you?"

Still wearing suspenders, the handsome man, with chiseled features and sexy aroma, gave that smile she remembered so clearly from the other day. It crossed his entire face. And now a twin smile of her own, crossed her face.

"Peaches!" he called as he hurried back. "Now I remember. It's just that you are out of context here in those clothes and on the boardwalk. I mistook you for a tourist."

"That must be it." Her heart floated with happiness as she sucked in her jiggly midsection.

He extended his hand then pointed over his shoulder at the Coffee Cafe. "By the way, I'm Leo."

"I'm a Capricorn."

"No, my name is Leo. Leo Stadler. Listen, I haven't had my morning coffee yet and cannot think without two cups. Join me?"

"Leo? Morning coffee? It's almost noon."

"I worked late and just got up." He held out his arm, chuckling. "Hey, you're a funny girl."

She took a few deep breaths. *Leo. What a perfect name. Much better than Benjamin.* Calmly she analyzed the situation, and like a lost kitten brought in from the heat of the day, she followed him to a table. He even pulled out a chair for her to sit, just like Pat Jenkins always did for his wife, whom he still referred to as his bride, even after fifty years of marriage. And who, probably by now, were both enjoying reading all kinds of erotic fiction.

"So, do you need coffee to get your brain going in the morning?"

"No. I don't even like coffee ice cream. I don't even

sell it."

"You must be an amazing woman then. But tell me how you function without it?" He laughed.

Captivated, she listened to the sound of his voice and when he had stopped, she answered. "I have Tilly."

"What's a Tilly?"

"Tilly is my cocker spaniel. She makes me walk her every morning for a mile. She's great company for me at home. Do you have a dog?"

"Of course, I do. Everyone should have some sort of pet. It helps us be kinder people."

Her surprise over seeing him on the boardwalk now melted into a comfortable conversation about ice cream and Mermaid Island and morning drinks. They were dog lovers together, totally enjoying what now had turned into a happy day. Hours later, they said their goodbyes and sealed it with a sideways hug and a forehead kiss.

Jemma had a dress to buy. And the matching shoes. And needed colorful matching earrings, that is, if Audrey had any. Perhaps a visit to the lingerie shop was overdue.

By the time she returned to her shop, which by now was bustling with patrons, her arms were filled with bags. "Wow, look at you. Busy."

"Wow, look at you. Shopping," Derek whined.

"What a crowd. I knew as soon as the air warmed, we'd get busy."

"You mean, I've been busy. Where have you been?" Derek asked, combing his fingers through his messy hair, clearly overwhelmed.

"I've just had the best day, so far." Jemma bubbled. "And it's about to get lots better."

"You bought the other place? Can I manage it for you?" he asked while reading the shop names on the bags she carried.

"It's already been bought. Not by me. And the nightmare I feared could be beginning."

"Ice cream?"

"But so far, the place is empty."

"And tell me about the shopping. I've never seen you with a single bag on your arm and there must be ten of them now."

"I met Leo. That's the first name of man from the other day. You know, the one who found my button? We bumped into one another on the boardwalk. We had coffee. Well, he had coffee. I drank lemon water. And ate a sandwich. I passed on dessert which was no easy task. We talked nearly this entire time. And guess what? He asked me out, so I did a wee bit of shopping."

"You were on a spontaneous date. You went shopping while I worked my ass off in here, alone."

"A date?" she hopefully gasped. "Do you really think having coffee is considered a date when you just run into a person on the boardwalk? Well, if so, then this girl is about have herself a second date."

"This is so not like you. You are not being responsible."

"Nay. Nay. But I am." She wiggled her index finger in the air. Then she pulled Derek into the backroom, out of earshot of the pictures. "You see, running into Leo today was kismet. And kismet is good. This girl right here, Jemma Louise Singleton, is about to have some fun for a change. In a new dress with shoes that match. Earrings too. And other stuff. Just this morning you complained to me about not having enough friends to go out with. Well, I might have a new friend. And we are going out. Tomorrow night."

Jemma gazed into the smallest bag, which held her new lace panties and lace bra wrapped in white tissue paper, just like the sexy women in Larisa Stewart's books always wore. Did this mean she was now one of them?

"Ah." Derek raised his brows. "You are using a new voice."

"What new voice?"

"A sexy new voice. Not so sure it fits you, but I'm willing to decide. Say something more. Go ahead, talk."

"It's time for me to go home and get ready."

"Didn't you say the date is for tomorrow?"

"Do you know nothing about preparations for a date?"

"Obviously not."

"Me either, because it's been so long, so I better get on it right away. My hair needs a trim. My nails need a manicure. I need to find a new perfume."

"Okay, okay, I get it," Derek protested.

"That means you close tonight and tomorrow."

"I don't know how to do the receipts." Derek scowled.

"You've seen me do them at least a hundred times. Time for you to learn, Mister Business Major."

Chapter 7

If the perfect night could be recreated from dreams, this would be it. Larisa Stewart would most certainly agree. First, the late evening sky was a giant sparkler catching the last rays of sunlight. Then the dark sky crept in, and it seemed as though it was littered with strings of Edwardian-era diamond necklaces. The finale was the moon, as it turned itself into a spotlight which gave into an eerie glow seen hovering between clouds.

Below, she sat with Mr. Love at First Sight, whom she now verbally referred to as "Leo." He told her how lovely she looked. Still, Jemma unexpectedly felt silly in the cute tropical summer dress and the dang shoes that now hurt her feet. The lace on her new lingerie was a bit itchy. Real comfort was her uniform, her pink-soled shoes, her stretched-out underwear, and her jewelry of choice, which would most likely be the nametag, *Hello, my name is Jemma*. However, this evening was the transition to an important change in her life starting with a new wardrobe, painful to wear or not. A new episode was beginning, and she'd call it "Finally, Love."

Jemma's fresh catch of the day was perfect, and the lobster dinner was delicious, too. Leo poured her fourth glass of wine. Like an octopus with tentacles, Jemma held onto it with nervous fingers. Conversation came slow and was mainly how wonderful the scent of salty air was, which made her wish she hadn't sprayed the new cologne across her bosom. Clearly the two aromas didn't mesh; she could tell from the way Leo coughed every time the wind was at her back. With her brain stuck on empty, she struggled to find the right balance of topics. Good at making to-do lists, she wondered why she didn't have one labeled "interesting topics." Most likely the answer lay in the preoccupation of struggling into her new dress, without sweet Audrey present to help. Jemma held out her glass. "More wine. Please."

"Another?" He slightly shook his head in disbelief.

"Please." Her jaws ached from smiling at him. It was both unnerving and thrilling to have a date for the first time in over a decade. Here she sat with a charming man, wearing a pretty dress, and she felt restless: unbalanced and unsure how to act. There were so many choices: woman of mystery? Aloof? Ready for romance? Should she carry the conversation? Share the conversation? Or ask questions about him? Was she speaking too loudly? Were her words stupid? Was dating really worth all these questions? She tried to catch a glimpse of how she looked in the wine glass. No luck.

"How long have you been managing the ice cream shop?" Leo asked, filling her glass, as she noted he still had plenty left in his.

"About fifteen years, alone."

"The Peach on the Beach was the bomb. Great marketing name."

"Thank you. That particular ice cream was created by me."

"You may have mentioned that. Sorry if I forgot. I hope you get a cut of the product's success since you created it."

"Not only did I create that flavor, but I also add

about six new flavors a year while filtering out the less popular. I am also the owner. It's my life's work." *Darn, that sounds so pathetic. Who's interested in a pathetic person? Certainly not Leo Stadler. Surely the women of the island regarded him as a prime catch.*

"Your gift to humanity." He held up his glass.

She wondered if this was a joke or a sincere compliment. So hard to tell these days, especially without dating practice. "Yea, I'm a regular Nemo of ice cream."

"You should be proud. Not easy to run a successful business, especially when the island counts on seasonal capital to survive."

"We do well, even in the off-season months. Although we make a bundle in the summer." *More wine. I need more wine. God of the universe, please make me witty and help me think of more things to say and nothing that sounds dumb.*

"Glad to hear it. Looks as though you need another refill?"

"We may need another bottle. Is this your first time on the island?" Jemma asked holding out her glass.

"This is my second visit. I planned on staying a week, but now I think I'll be staying a bit longer."

"Longer. Sounds so nice." *I wonder if I'm using my sexy voice or just a drunken voice?*

"It should be prosperous." He seemed so sure of himself.

"How so? Do tell me how staying longer makes it more prosperous." She laughed into her empty glass.

"I think you've had plenty of wine." He unwrapped her fingers from around the glass and set it back on the table.

"Where's home?" Her tongue felt lithe. A calm feeling draped over her. It felt good that wine was settling her nerves.

"Usually a city. In an apartment for now."

Jemma stared into his eyes, remembering an article she recently read that if a couple stared into one another eyes for twenty minutes, they'd fall in love. She wondered if it was possible. Why not give it a try?

"Sounds as though you travel a lot."

"At times." He pulled at his open collar and looked at the ocean. "There's nothing more important than having dinner with a beautiful woman, on an open patio, while listening to the waves."

Leo made her feel like a diamond. "You must have an interesting occupation to travel a lot."

"Just like everyone else, I'm always up for something new and fresh."

"What about a wife?" She congratulated herself for asking such a brave question, but it was one she most needed an answer to.

"Never married. You?" He leaned back.

"Same."

Jemma ran her hand through her already-reshaped, done by an actual hairstylist, windblown hair and made a mental note to focus on Leo.

"So, does wishing for something new and fresh translate into changing careers often?"

"I'm way too boring. I'd rather know more about you." He waved away her question.

"If I talk more than five minutes, you probably know all there is to know."

"I highly doubt that. I'd say there are many layers of flavors to you. I may take my time in getting to know them."

She felt her cheeks warming. He moved his chair closer, drew her chin to his lips. As they kissed, her mind dissolved all thoughts, as she matched his intensity. Her brain released chemicals, igniting pleasure centers in her body. She felt euphoric, fanning feelings of affection. Her stress level bottomed out. Afterwards she panted, while trying to catch her breath. For a long moment, they stared into one another's eyes, before sitting back into their seats.

"I've never been kissed like that," she whispered.

"I hope you enjoyed it as much as I did."

"Of course."

Leo picked up his fork and fed her a piece of his lobster dripping in butter.

She caught a drip with her napkin.

"You are quite a woman. Tell me about your life. I want to know everything."

"Everything?" Her eyes widened.

"Everything," he reassured her.

"That'll take about five minutes," Jemma reminded him. "What you see is what you get. Nothing much has changed in my life in the last fifteen years, since returning to the island."

"Ah, so you haven't spent your entire life here. Where did you return from?" Leo seemed eager to know.

"New Orleans. I went to culinary school. That's where I learned a lot about blending flavors."

"You must be a good cook." Again, he took her hand as though he couldn't stop from touching her.

Seeing her hand placed in his, she became aware of the obvious stares from other tables. Surely, he noticed it too. It made her happy he wasn't ashamed to show affection so publicly.

The wine. His warm hand. The salty air peppered with her cologne, made her momentarily dizzy. She drew deep, even breaths to regain her equilibrium.

"I can turn on an oven, but my focus has always been on creating ice cream dishes. Top priority. I'm darn lucky to own my business, yet with that ownership comes a new package of problems. Each difficult situation must be greeted with a smile, while I tamp down my panic and come up with a solution."

"Are you telling me that you are unhappy in your career as the boss of the only worthy ice cream shop on the island? If you are, move onto something new."

"I love what I'm doing. Really. But it's not always smooth sailing. Enough of me. More of you, please."

"There's not much more to say. I contract work. Locations and projects change according to the need. Besides it's a lovely evening, and the food was good. Rather, it was great. Look at us, nothing left unless we lick our plates."

Jemma giggled and wondered if he would actually do that. And if he did, would she still be interested? Of course, she would.

"Are you staying at the Mermaid Island Hotel?"

"No, as a matter of fact, I recently rented a cottage. Small, but suits my immediate purpose."

"Which is where?" The conversation went dead. Jemma was a bit uncomfortable over the silence which unexpectedly ensued. Time for a follow-up question. "I thought all the rentals were booked early last season. Or did one become available?"

"Maybe the latter. I rent the small blue, one-room cottage behind the ice cream shop. Not yours, the new shop. I believe the word you used to describe it was 'braggy.'"

"Oh." Jemma withdrew her from hand from his.

Leo's expression wrinkled. His brown eyes dimmed. So much for her plan to be cheery, but he stepped onto a sore subject, and her reaction nearly ruined her best evening, ever.

"How about dessert?" He occupied himself with the menu.

"I was just thinking the same thing. How about ice cream?" She leaned forward and pulled on his menu, slowly batting her new false eyelashes just like the heroine Amanda Givings did in *Love Is Everywhere*. "I know a place that makes the best specialty ice cream in the entire world, not just on this island."

"But it's closed at this hour, right?" Abruptly, his eyes smiled.

"Not if you know the owner. And I have the keys."

"You know the owner? You have the keys?"

"Yes, and yes." It was so much fun acting playful.

They walked arm in arm down the boardwalk. The night air carried their conversation along with music from the bandstand playing on the pier. By the time they reached the shop door, the air was chilly, and they looked forward to warming up inside. Hoping Leo's arms would be the heated appendages she needed, Jemma fished for keys in her purse. She held them up to show they had been found, then she turned the lock and Leo opened the door, allowing her to step in first. Jemma turned on the backroom light but made sure the door was locked behind them, with the CLOSED sign planted firmly facing out in the window.

Still feeling the wine effect, she dizzily scooted

around the counter and asked with a loud giggle, "What flavor is your fancy?"

"Peach on the Beach, of course."

"You've come to the right place then."

Choosing to sit where the Jenkinses sat on Mondays, Jemma drew the curtains. She wasn't afraid to be alone in this old building with this man she hardly knew. Not only was his demeanor gentle, but she also had her ancestors watching over her. She smiled across the room at them.

Now she looked into Leo's face straight on, noting the details, finding him even more handsome; his dark hair was threaded with gray, cropped short, yet messy from the evening wind; strong features with a straight and narrow nose. A day's stubble ran along his jawline which she wanted to reach across the table and kiss. His voice was comfortably pitched like a room you wanted to move into and remain.

"More ice cream, handsome?" The words trembled in her mouth. Before he could answer, she was on her feet and wove her way across the room, between the crowded tables. Hoping he was watching, she slowed down a little, moving lazily, as if she were bored. Then, as she turned to face him, she leaned her back at the edge of the counter. It was then she felt herself sobering up while experiencing feelings she hoped to explore with this man.

Leo rose to his feet. His gaze took her in from head to toe, causing her to suck in her stomach and wishing she had worn two panty shapers instead of just one. She locked eyes with his gaze. He let loose a suggestive chuckle, as he came toward her. Jemma filled with anticipation. They stood toe to toe. "More Peach on the

Beach?"

"Maybe it's time to sample something else." He tugged the right dress strap down from her shoulder, then began leaving a trail of kisses. Electricity surged through her body, eliciting a deep sigh. How she wanted him to taste not only her lips but her cleavage too. What a grand, swirling feeling this was, coursing through every fiber of her being. It'd be so easy to lean back and give into this exciting new desire that heated her body, but her head said it was too soon. After all, it was just the second date and on the very same day too. It'd be terrible to be termed a loose woman so soon. Just as in Larisa Stewart's book *The Day He Left*, Leo would pack to leave the island— make that Oliver leaving the city—and all that was left was an empty room, and Angela's empty heart—make that Jemma's empty heart.

"I know just the ice cream." She ducked under his arm and scooped Devil's Delight into a paper cup. She set it on the same spot where he had placed the button. She lifted her sticky fingers to her lips pantomiming some show she saw on TV. She hoped it was a sexy move on her part and not laughable like a comedy show.

Whatever happened to that button, anyway? More unrelated thoughts tumbled through her mind, such as, *maybe I should buy more buttons, but will it be difficult to match? I can always just pin the top, so my cleavage doesn't show. Or do I really want it to show?* "You don't seem too interested in that ice cream. If you don't eat it soon, it'll melt."

Leo put his arms around her. Moving into him, she rested her head on his shoulder. She swallowed back the imperceptible tremor in her voice. "Are you taking advantage of my generous ice cream ways?"

After a few tries of picking her up, he finally was able to seat her on the counter. She didn't want to break the spell between them by informing him that he had just placed her in the cup of ice cream.

As Leo ran his hand through her red hair, which was in disarray about her shoulders, she felt the cold melting of ice cream between her buttocks. He kissed her gently. His hand slowly drifted between her legs, up her dress, lightly pinching her inner thighs, causing her insides to curl. It embarrassed her, hearing herself groan and feel her breath uncontrollably catching. His warm breath caressed her skin, his hip against hers, with his hand guiding her body. There was that matter of the sticky ice cream she decided not to address. It was impossible to separate her wetness from the ice cream's. She wondered how to catch this moment in a new ice cream flavor. Island Indiscretion, she'd name it. She leaned back against the wall mirror, her purposeful seductive pose in full display, and slid her private parts to the edge of the counter for easy access, hearing the cup hit the floor, which drew his gaze downward. This was fun. Reputation be damned.

"We better go." Abruptly he stepped back.

"We, what? Oh yes, of course." She sat up and jumped off the counter without his help. *What went wrong? I know: he felt the roll of fat I have going on beneath my boobs. Plus, I was too eager. And I was too willing on our first ever date. What have I done? What must he think of me?* "I had a great time. Thanks for everything. You go on, I'll lock up." She waved him toward the door, defaulting to businesslike demeanor.

"No. I'm driving you home," Leo insisted, taking her hand.

"No, I can drive myself." Not wanting to be hurt, she pulled back and promptly walked away.

"You didn't drive this evening. I picked you up." He caught her by the hand and kissed the back of it. "I'll see you home."

"Okay." She grabbed her purse and tried to nonchalantly dislodge the ice cream cup that by now was wedged into the heel of her new shoe. Without success, she clumped across the room with it still firmly stuck. Outside Leo gently extracted the cup and tossed it into an empty bin.

As they slid into the car next to each other, he leaned in for a kiss. It was soft. Quick. Without emotional savoriness. Then Leo pulled her closer and kissed her again. The second kiss meant business causing her mind to reel with zesty ice cream palatableness. "I really enjoyed this evening with you. Let's do this again, if that's okay."

Jemma responded with a particular smile that silently meant "perhaps." In a similar novel situation, *When Love Finds You Vol. 2*, Larisa Stewart described the scene so well, that Jemma felt certain she copied the smile of the lead female character, Karon Carmichael.

At home, the freshly kissed entrepreneur changed into a stretched-out night shirt and sat on the front porch beneath the bug lamp to write another letter to her favorite romance author, about tonight's events. Atmosphere be damned.

Dear Larisa,

You not only pen romantic love scenes, but your books are filled with dating tips which I intend to put into good use, whatever chance I get. You asked about my sexuality, well, I've found someone who makes me come alive in that way. I actually feel pretty when I am with him. I find myself wanting the kind of life I had a long time ago before I returned to this island. Filled with confidence. Expectations of love. Yet, I'm still riddled with doubts of what tomorrow may bring.

Falling in love for the first time,
Jemma

Then she slipped the letter into her usual pink envelope, addressed it in care of the publisher and stamped it.

Still awake, Jemma began to plot.

Chapter 8

Orbs floated like Roman candles about the bedroom. The aura appeared as blue twilight. Since sleep eluded her, Jemma sat up and wrapped the wool blanket around her shoulders. The room grew colder as each orb entered. They hadn't materialized yet, and she was pretty sure they'd take their time to achieve a more dramatic effect, which she braced for. Family meetings were never easy. Tonight, she was clearly awake and reached for her cell to take pictures of the magic which lit up her room. This would be proof enough for Sara to believe her.

Several orbs now changed colors from candle glow to black as they gained energy to convey their messages, while two others remained translucent reflecting playfulness. Her ancestors whispered to one another in a language she didn't comprehend. Jemma waited patiently, but right now, by the sound of the voices, they were quibbling, which only meant trouble for her.

One by one, they became an unidentifiable shape then formed into the body they were known as when alive. Great-Great-Uncle Ralph was the first, followed by the twins Great-Aunt Vera and Great-Aunt Bessie. Last came Great-Great-Great-Grandfather Harold, again, which meant this was no social call. All together like this, they never made friendly calls. This was considered business of the serious kind.

"What brings you here tonight?" Jemma yawned,

hoping they'd see how tired she was and make it short. "The shop is doing quite well, as you must already know."

"Are you on course to find out more about the new ice cream shop on the boardwalk?" Harold pointedly asked as he stood at the foot of the bed.

"I've always been on course. Never veering." Jemma disguised hurt feelings by acting self-assured.

"Three days have passed since my singular visit. Tell us what you've found?" Harold demanded.

"Well, nothing so far. You don't want the entire island community finding out that we are concerned. Right? Gotta take things slow."

"Slow? If I were alive, and running the place, I would have been on top of this, and those new people never would've stepped foot on my island. In fact, by this time, I'd not only be running the parlor but also their place."

"I do understand how upset you are. I will for sure find out more today," Jemma promised looking at the clock, it read 3:33 a.m.

"We think you are sidetracked. As in preoccupied," Ralph stated, as he twisted himself into a funnel shape that whirled. "Wheeee, this is sure fun."

"Sidetracked? I'm working twelve hours a day." Jemma reasoned.

"That's not the sidetracked we meant, dear." Great-Aunt Bessie floated above the dresser while fixing her hair in a mirror, which didn't hold her image.

"And we weren't going to say anything, but we noticed the button-popping incident, the other day," Great-Aunt Vera scoffed as she took off her sweater and hung it in the air. "Very undignified."

"Downright embarrassing," Jemma agreed.

"We also noticed you haven't yet sewn the button back on. Stay buttoned up to the chin, my dear," Bessie sweetly spoke, tapping her fingers beneath her chin. "Keep them guessing till the wedding night."

"The only reason we are mentioning it now is we saw you two together in the shop," Vera continued.

"Acting unbecoming of a lady," Harold sneered. "Blackening our good name."

"But I like Leo. I am thinking he might like me too."

"Holy hogwash. You need to keep your eye on the business. It's been about three days in your time since I gave you the first instructions." Harold began to fade but came back as dark as ever. "It's hard holding on tonight, something is getting in the way, making me fade."

"Is it your heart, dear Jemma?" Bessie asked Jemma. "I remember what it's like to fall in love. Maybe your positive energy is putting out his negative energy."

"Bessie, close your mouth. I am the only one in charge. Listen to me, Jemma. We have placed on your shoulders a gem of a shop that's now yours. You and the island have profited well by it. But you are allowing emotions to get in the way. Stay on top of things."

A great wind jutted from between his lips causing everyone's hair to blow straight back. "Men nowadays are up to no good. They aren't made of grit and fire like back in my day. They get manicures and shave off their hair. My mother fell in love with a prissy philanderer."

"We never heard about that." Vera held a blue and red tin toy whistle trying to make it whistle, but it made no sound. Jemma wondered if she took it off Latimer.

"And just how do you think I got here, then? Well, not here, here, where we are, but here, there, where you are. I refuse to refer to him as my father. My mother raised me alone. We don't want you to have to raise a child by yourself."

"The island gossip would be awful." Ralph returned to his body formation and wiggled his thick brows.

"This was my first day off in a year. I think I'm entitled to that."

"You know nothing about that man, Leo. He could be another island scoundrel. Waiting to take advantage of you. Do not trust him. Our business here tonight is three-fold: Number one is to protect you. So, get rid of all distractions like Leo. Number two is to protect the business. Number three is to boot that other shop off the island. Until all this is taken care of you take zero days off. We didn't take days off, did we, Ralph?"

"Not at all, but fun can be good. After all, you only live once." He snickered as he removed his upper teeth to look at.

"Not while the business is in competition. We must remain the sole distributor of ice cream on Mermaid Island. Go out and find who bought the shop. You need to know the owner's name. Is there a manager, and if so, who? Find the supplier. Let me warn you. If you do not heed my words, you will be dealing with Eli."

"Eli?" Jemma quivered at the sound of his name. Actually, it was the sound of his name how Harold said it. "Who is Eli?"

"Eli is my older brother and can be dangerous."

"We keep him under wraps," Bessie explained politely.

"Eli will step in very soon if we don't bring to him the answers he needs," Harold said.

Jemma gasped. "Will he hurt me?"

"No. Not in the way you are thinking." Harold looked around. "Time to go. Now everyone. Remember what I said, Jemma, remember." As if zapped by an electric shock, Harold disappeared in a flash of light.

"Mind the business, but remember to have fun too." Ralph laughed and spun himself into a ball and tumbled out the window.

Vera dropped the tin toy whistle, but she couldn't find it again. She shrugged in defeat. "We are on your side, Toots." She curled back into an orb and spun about the room, then vanished. Bessie was the last to go. "I so wish your mother was here to guide you instead of a bunch of crusty old dead men. Listen to your heart. We love you. If you need us, we will come back for girl talk."

"I love you, too. Even Harold. Maybe someday I'll meet everyone." Jemma waved goodbye to Bessie, as she too returned to an orb and floated quietly out the window.

Sleep was always difficult to come by when these visits occurred. A lot of left-over energy remained in the room. Sometimes it took days for it to dissipate. At least Tilly always slept through it, which seemed strange. But the cocker spaniel was sleeping peacefully next to her. Tomorrow she'd be so filled with energy that it'd be hard to get the pup inside.

And then she woke up. Daylight streamed through the window. The clock showed it was eight o'clock. Jemma hadn't been aware of falling asleep. But there she was under white cotton sheets with the edges of the covers tucked in all the way around the bed, making it impossible to move.

"Why do you always do this to me on your visits?" Jemma yelled. She closed her eyes and could hear the roll of the ocean. The call of the seagulls. Bit by bit she was able to work a foot out from the covers. Then a leg. Soon she set herself free. She looked at it as a loving gesture of saying goodnight and making sure she was safely tucked in, although it was ninety humid degrees already. But that bunch sure had a way of freezing up the place.

She followed Tilly from bed and leaned over the bathroom sink to look in the mirror. Where her hair had been soft and flowy the night before, it was now like a thick coarse dish-scrub pad.

The phone jolted Jemma from her thoughts.

"Are you okay?"

"Yes, I'm fine. I overslept. I'm getting dressed as we speak." Jemma pulled a fresh uniform from the closet. Something in his voice chilled her. "Open the shop."

"I don't think that's a good idea."

"Why? Is that all you are going to say?"

"For now. Just get here."

On her way out the door, Jemma remembered using her cell to take pictures of the orbs. Pausing to look for them, she decided to take them to Sara for proof this morning. As she scrolled through the photos, she couldn't locate them. Panicked, she scrolled up and down several times. They had to be the last pictures on her cell, only those were of Tilly, taken two days ago. Jemma checked her trash. Then the cloud. Nothing. "They aren't real. I imagine them, like Sarah said. What a horrid nightmare." Giving a backwards look at the bed and remembering how the covers had been tucked tightly about her, she again wasn't so sure it wasn't a dream.

Chapter 9

Jemma's body buzzed like someone died. The sound of Derek's cell, calling her for the second time, sent shock waves through her body. Adrenaline surged as she pressed the gas pedal harder, careening dangerously around sharp coastal corners. In minutes she traveled along the flat roadway toward the beach, dreading to find out what waited at the shop. Up ahead was her empty parking spot where she turned, and there Derek sat waiting on the back steps. The car in park, the ignition keys in hand, she hurried across the pavement.

"Was there a fire? A break-in? Someone die?"

Derek unfurled himself and gave a half wave as he slowly walked to meet her. This was a huge change from the normally gregarious person she knew.

"You look rattled." She searched his eyes for answers.

"We are dealing with a whole lot more than just crooked pictures this morning."

"What's wrong?" Her skin prickled. "AC go out? Ice cream melt? What?"

"None of the above. I think I may owe you an apology. I hate to ask you this, but first I need to know. Did you have a visit from your ancestors last night?" Derek asked.

"What? You made it sound like an emergency just to ask me about old photographs? Do you realize how panicked I was on my way here? I could have driven off a cliff." Jemma took a deep breath to settle herself.

"It is still an important matter."

Jemma noticed fear in his eyes. Not wanting islanders to see them in a panic she took his elbow and walked him inside.

Derek blocked the doorway into the parlor.

"Tell me." Jemma prepared herself for what Derek was about to say.

"*All-lll* the pictures are crooked this morning. Some are barely hanging."

"You know yourself this happens often." Then Jemma remembered Harold's warning concerning Eli. An eerie calm settled around them. "It's not just the pictures this time?"

"It's worse." Derek breathed deeply.

"Anything broken?" Repairing old wooden frames was difficult and finding the antique wavy glass nearly impossible.

"None of the pictures are broken."

"That's a relief to hear because my ancestors aren't happy with me right now." Jemma shivered, not sure how much to divulge. Certainly nothing about Eli. A silence in the air made her dread walking further. Nevertheless, she had no choice. Jemma gently pushed Derek to the side and stepped into the center of the main room. A crunching sound beneath her feet made her look down where she stood in a sea of shattered glass. Sunshine glared from the mirror shards. Her knees buckled slightly at the once mirrored wall, now in need of drywall. The very spot where Leo had set her on the counter, the same mirror she lamented over her appearance in daily, somehow had shattered and brought down the wall with it. Her throat dried. It took a bit to find the words and make her voice heard. "Damnit. How did this happen?"

"No idea. The shop was like this when I got here. I checked the windows and the door. No damage to entry and all tightly locked from the inside. I figured you had another family meeting? What precipitated the visitation this time?"

"My date with Leo, among other things." Her face blushed. She pictured herself in the pretty new dress, with the shoulder strap off her shoulder. Leo moving his hands up her thighs. Their deep kisses leading to groans of pleasure. "The shop will remain closed until we have a chance to thoroughly clean, which includes tossing all the open drums of ice cream in the front display. I can't take a chance that some of the glass penetrated them."

Jemma tiptoed around the mess on the floor, then stopped to stare into the faces of generations of family members. She fell quiet for a time while tapping her toe against the marble floor. Heatedly she spat at once, "I know one or more of you are responsible for doing this. Speak up. Which ones? Who? Okay. Silent now, huh? Don't have anything to say to me. Cowards. You sure had plenty to say the other night. Every one of you is destroying the business you say you love. Eli? How about you? Harold, what can you tell me?"

"Are you crazy? Should you be confronting them like this?" Derek sounded aghast and tugged her arm. "And who is Eli?"

"What? You now believe me? Or is this a joke?" Jemma flooded with fury and spoke accusingly.

"No joke," Derek admitted as he crossed his heart. "I believe you."

"Why now?" She demanded to know.

"This was no break-in with the locks set and the alarm still armed. Settle. I am on your side."

"Really? You have no idea what this means to me to hear you say this. So, you've come to the dark side?" She did her best to joke but knew it fell short, especially she said it through falling tears. "Earlier, you mentioned an apology."

"This is the first time I've seen the pictures in such total disarray. Plus, the broken mirror. The wall! Its dust all over the room. That's a new one. You've told me these stories about night hauntings. Previously, I thought the picture slippage was due to atmospheric conditions and the ghostly meetings were part of your island schtick. That's what I apologize for, plus thinking you were some crackpot lady." He nervously chuckled.

Unexpectedly, they burst into laughter, released from pent-up fear. "Glad you've come over to the crazy side with me. You believe me, but my therapist still doesn't."

"Then she should be fired," he jested. "Anyone who doesn't believe you should be banished from the island."

"You might be right. Most families bicker about who gets the silver, or how many presents more someone else got for Christmas, or who Grandpa's favorite is. Not me. I get family pictures that come to life and pay visits. My life has been reduced to this—hauntings. But in a way, my life has also been enriched by them."

"Turns out you're a smart girl." Derek put his arm around her shoulder. "Buck up. I'm totally on your side now."

"Thanks, Derek, for finally understanding. I need someone on my side besides Tilly."

"Always the jokester. I gotta come clean. Once I thought your wild imaginings could be taken care with medication."

"Wouldn't that be great? My life simplified by meds." Jemma stepped aside and took a moment for herself as Derek picked the closed sign up from the floor and secured it in the window.

It was then she knew she'd not return to see Sara professionally again. It became crystal clear they each were influenced by personal experiences, neither willing to accept the other's point of view. There was a real disconnect. Jemma didn't realize until that moment; until she walked into this mess, that sitting across from Sara in that calm room, their lives were not connected. They existed on opposite poles. Sara had no distractions in her life, no extra noise, nothing eating up the empty spaces in her thoughts. Jemma's anger and loss were too raw for Sara to comprehend. But out of acceptance, and time, and distance and loss, she came to this one simple conclusion; it was better to believe in something, than nothing.

"You are no longer alone. I'm with you, babe." Derek gave her an unexpected squeeze.

"Thanks. But I don't want you getting involved in these family arguments. Hey, did you just call me 'babe'?"

"Yeah, babe. You've been strutting your stuff and looking hot these past few days since Mr. Whatchamacallit showed."

"Really? Do you think he noticed me strutting my stuff? Never mind." She playfully strutted back to the broken mirror, which resembled glitter. "I'm not replacing that wall of mirrors. I know it makes this space look larger, but it also makes me look larger too. What are your thoughts of a mirror ball instead?"

"I'm thinking the era is 70s disco. Not in keeping with the early 1900s look." Derek studied the frozen picture faces as Jemma straightened the frames. "They aren't a friendly-looking bunch. I bet holidays and family gatherings were a bitch."

"They are." Jemma gave a shrug.

"You celebrate holidays with them too?" Derek seemed amazed.

"Sometimes. Goodness only knows that when the family gets fired up, nothing stops them."

"It's almost as if they walk out of the pictures, causing them to swing off the nails." Derek tucked his hands under his armpits.

"You seem nervous."

"Today I was the first one who walked in on the mess. Be patient with me," he said reflectively. "It's my first haunting."

"The sixty-fifth haunting is as scary as the first."

"Why not just remove the pictures from the wall? Let's trash them." Derek reached for the closest frame.

"Whoa. I'd hate to think about the repercussions. Besides, tourists and the Mermaid Island Historical Society like having these in this building. It's the only building never bulldozed by strong hurricane winds. It's the lone original building standing."

"Tradition?"

"Exactly." Jemma patted Derek's arm.

"I'm intrigued. Tell me about your relatives." Derek stepped closer to the yard-long photograph and studied the faces. "I'll pay attention this time."

"Starting on the far left with my great-great-great-grandfather Harold Singleton in his wheelchair, taken right before his death. But you should see him now. He gets around just fine. The family business began with him when he was a teen. Strong and healthy at that point in his life, he handmade a wooden cart and filled it with blocks of ice and then hand churned ice cream, which he sold for a penny a cone." Jemma continued with the story, leap frogging over the stories of family members she didn't know. Then Jemma worked her way around the wall of faces in different frames, some standing alone, some with spouses, some with siblings, others with children. "All were dedicated to making a success of this business. I wish I knew everyone's stories. I keep a notebook on those I do. Most I've never met in life, but boy, do they ever show up when I take a wrong step."

"Wrong step? Like, living your own life? Come here every day and check for crooked pictures after a haunting? Is this really what you want to do until you're a floating orb? Or is there something else?"

"The family business is tradition."

"I hate to say this, but you seem to be held hostage by a bunch of dead people."

A cold wind swam through her body. It was as though she felt suspended with strings attached to her legs and arms. Looking up into cloud-like puffs, there were her ancestors pulling at the strings. She spun about and faced Derek. "You are right. I never thought of it that way."

"So here you are, alone with me, still making their dreams come true."

"We are making their dreams come true. You and I are profiting."

"But what's your dream, Jemma?"

"Someone else recently asked me that question. I really don't know. Hey, let me take a picture of you, okay? I think there's something wrong with my camera. It's not holding my pictures."

"Of course. Shall I pose?"

"If you wish."

Derek crossed his eyes and stuck out his tongue. As Jemma held out her cell, sounds of heavy footsteps plunked across the wooden backroom floor. Derek's face dropped, and he froze in place. "Oh my God. They're back?"

"If they are, it's the first time they've come during daylight hours and on heavy feet. Floating in bubbles is their usual mode of transportation." Jemma tucked her phone into her pocket.

"Anyone here?" Leo knocked on the door jamb, then walked into the parlor. "Your front door is locked while the backdoor is standing open. Everything okay?"

Jemma turned to see him. Genuine happiness glowed in her cheeks and sparkled in her eyes. And just like that, she was no longer afraid. She knew everything would be all right.

Chapter 10

"I'll start cleaning up the mess. Now where is the broom and dustpan?" Derek went in search of cleaning supplies.

"Jemma, what happened? Was there a break-in?" Leo's voice filled with concern. He took her hands. Leo's soothing touch temporarily washed out to sea the worry she carried about her family. Being with Leo was all that mattered. And then she remembered. Her family didn't like him. Even suspected him of high ice cream crimes. Their ire focused on him. She withdrew from him and took a giant step back. Had their affectionate interaction been noticed?

Not wanting to explain the complicated truth, she opted for an easy answer. "Not real sure yet exactly what happened, but we will figure it out."

"You will figure this out? Isn't that the police's job? Wait. Shouldn't the Island police be called before you clean up what could be evidence?" Leo asked as he watched Derek emerge with a vacuum.

"I think it's best if Derek and I handle things our own way." Jemma turned from his penetrating gaze, not wanting him to see the lie in her eyes.

"Let me help with this mess." Leo reached for the vacuum.

"Nothing here I can't handle. If you want to help, take Jemma somewhere for the day. Look at her, she's shook."

"Really, Derek, I'm fine. Leo, I need to stay. Call me later?"

Derek pulled her to the side. "What you need to do is to leave and take lover boy with you. The family watches." He nodded toward the wall.

"These are desperate times. Harold says I'm slacking and wants me to find out all sorts of information about the new ice cream shop. I need to get that done today," she whispered. "If I put it off any longer, there'll be hell to pay. Literal hell to pay."

"Let me take care of that," Derek promised.

"Are you sure?"

"Yes. Let me do this for you."

"You are really stepping up lately." Jemma pulled the list from her pocket. "These are the things we need to find out about the shop. There must be some strategy in knowing all this, if only I knew what it was."

"Leave it to me." Derek pushed Jemma and Leo toward the back. "Go, have some fun, you kids. I've got this. If anything, unexpected happens, I'll text you, Jemma."

Leo led Jemma to his sports convertible. "Peaches, I know just the place to take you."

"Where's that?" She cocked her head to the side.

"It's midmorning. I'm starved, and I bet you haven't eaten yet today, either. First, we'll stop for snacks. Then I'll take you to my favorite spot." He spun the car around and headed out of the bay.

"I thought my shop was your favorite island spot," she teased. "And a picnic in my uniform? Nay. I need to change first."

"No time. We are on our way to a happy, carefree

day. Just stopping at the market while you wait in the car and relax. I'll be right out."

It was a scorcher of the day, and not even eleven in the morning. Leo carried two shopping bags of groceries to the car. After depositing them into the trunk, they drove up the palm-tree-lined coastline, then headed inland, where the air was cooler. After crossing over the first bridge, Jemma sat up straighter to get a sense of where they headed. Off in the distance to the left was a sheltered water area. A little farther out, shrimp boats were making their way back to the harbor with morning catch. A breeze filled the air. Red flower bushes waved from the roadside. "You've only been here a few times on vacation and already have a favorite spot?" Jemma wondered aloud.

"That I do." He pulled to a stop near the lookout. "I have a blanket for us to sit on. Come."

Jemma took a deep breath, along with his hand, and got out of the car. It was then she felt her body shaper had rolled down into her belly. It made her wrestle with it, pulling it back up to right under her boobs, resulting in a most smooth effect.

Together they carried the bags; the blanket slung over Leo's shoulders. As he walked, she followed through a weed worn path. At the cliff top, Leo spread the blanket as she made herself comfortable on it. "I've lived here all my life, but somehow missed this particular view. It's gorgeous."

"I knew you'd like it. And off-islanders can find spots that residents never pay attention to."

"Those are fighting words. Don't let another resident hear you speak them."

One by one, he removed groceries as if presenting

them to her for final approval. Grapes. Various cheeses already cut and placed on a charcuterie board under cellophane. A bottle of wine with a screw top. Two plastic cups. Chicken salad with specialty crackers. Chocolate-covered strawberries. "I hope I haven't forgotten anything."

"By the looks of this spread, you haven't. This is perfect. Thank you." Jemma felt quite flirty even in her uniform, marveling over how an hour earlier she was in the depths of despair and now felt extremely exhilarated. Trying to be funny, Jemma made a cooing sound but suddenly choked.

Quickly Leo poured the wine and handed her the cup. "I guess I should've brought water. Sorry."

The apology was dismissed by a wave of her hand.

"Feeling better?" He squeezed her leg.

She nodded. Leo smiled warmly. His eyes centered on her. In this moment she was completely happy that an unexpected laugh bubbled up that couldn't be stifled. "So, you refer to yourself as an off-islander."

"Isn't that the correct term for someone who spends most of their life on the mainland?"

"You're so real." She smiled.

"You mean, real-ly silly."

"No. You are real. No fakery."

Slowly she sipped at the wine, not wanting to gulp it like she had at dinner. Always reflective, or self-accusing of her shortcomings, she didn't want to make a mistake or be perceived a social failure. She hoped he regarded her as girlfriend material. His girlfriend, someday. If only she had the courage of one of Larisa Stewart's heroines. Perhaps, this was a good time to figuratively step into the skin of one of the novel's characters. Which character should she choose? Quickly, she decided against doing so because today she needed to be herself. Leo liked she was real. It gave her something to build on. Today she remained Jemma, in her white uniform, with pink shoes, and nametag on her bust. Maybe, it'd be okay to remove the nametag, for today. And so she did. Years ago, she made peace with her size, and Leo definitely seemed comfortable with it. She opted to be none other than Jemma Louise Singleton, a pretty-faced woman filled with confidence, charm, and wit.

They slowly ate, enjoying the silence of being together. This man was exciting. Intelligent and complicated. Leo made her laugh. Lifted her spirits. But perhaps that's what relationships were all about. Not the fast hurried kind she read about. If she was willing to be herself and give it time, perhaps she'd be loved. It was okay to take things slowly.

"How long will you be on Mermaid Island?" Jemma asked breaking the silence.

"As soon as my work is finished."

"Which is?"

"Research." He winked.

"Interesting. Then you are a biologist? Oh wait, a contractor of some kind?"

"I'm a contractor of the boring kind." Leo rolled his eyes.

"And a master of deflection. I have yet to get a straight answer from you." Jemma pulled apart a clump of grapes.

"I'll do better. Ask another question. I promise I will give a straight-forward answer," Leo promised, crossing his heart.

"What about your ambitions and interests? Your aspirations?"

"Wow, such deep questions. I wasn't expecting an interrogation." Leo seemed truly stunned.

Jemma wondered if she caught him off guard about a secret he might be hiding. She came up with a lighthearted remark as she patted his stomach. "I enjoy interrogating people. Namely you."

"Okay, seriously, my ambition is to be the best at whatever my career might be at any given moment."

"Sounds to me as though you change careers frequently." Jemma supposed he just could be between those ambitious careers. "Go on."

"My present interest is you."

"Great answer." She squeezed his knee.

"And lastly, my aspiration is to buy a boat. Was down at the dock earlier today looking at some that Andy at the surf shop has up for sale."

"Somehow, I can't see you as the captain of a boat. But the driver of that sports car you have, definitely." She cupped her hand above her eyes to block the reflection of the sun coming off the water.

"I must admit, you intrigue me." He playfully touched the end of her nose.

"How so?" In turn, she batted his finger away pretending it was an insect.

"You're the most interesting female I've ever known."

"I thank you for that. And how long will your work here on the island last?" It felt as though she was playing a game of Clue with this man, watching for red flags. Each piece of information helped her discern his character. What was his intent? Her gut told her to be careful, but her heart yelped, "Full steam ahead."

"Let's enjoy this moment. Not run ahead and not look behind. Let's be present."

She lifted her eyebrows and sighed with frustration over his lack of information. Leo touched his lips to hers and slowly parted her mouth with his tongue, entering it. Leo scooted even closer until their bodies touched. His kisses were confident. But he was playing with her fire. When he sat back to stare at her, she touched her fingers to her lips, drinking in the powerful touch of his lips, reveling over how it transformed her. Then she returned to his mouth and his well-kissed lower lip.

He tugged her hair before breaking the kiss. And just like that, she came up with a new ice cream flavor name: Kissable Lips. She'd create a strawberry-cherry delight with fresh cream. All the ingredients would come from the island. As she was coming up with more ingredients, he began talking about how he loved Mermaid Island and wish he could stay forever. He pushed the hair from her eyes as thoughts of ice cream flavors melted.

Acting less drunk with wine and a lot more on passion, Leo began, once more, to kiss her. Slowly. Gaining speed. His lips pulling on hers. Her lips responding. Deep long kisses. His hands reached for her uniform buttons. He slowly moved his leg between her legs and his fingers finished unbuttoning her top. His hands felt refrigerator cold against her skin as he slid them beneath her bra, squeezing her breast. Although the struggle to get there was a bit difficult because the elastic was a bit tight. A text came in on her phone, then another and another.

"Sounds like you're needed, Peaches." He sat back on his elbows.

"Sorry, just one, one moment." Jemma looked down at the text. "It's Derek. I need to take this. Sorry. It'll just take a second."

—You are ruining one of the most perfect moments in my life. It better be good. —

—Sorry fluff bunny but I got some information I thought was important to you but I guess it can wait while you get screwed. —

—No, sorry. Is it about the new shop? Tell me. Who is buying it? —

—They are represented by a New York law firm who will not disclose the owner's name but they are handling the sale. —

—New York? Handling? You mean it's not a done deal? There's a sign. —

—They jumped the gun and now it's a legal matter because they already took possession of the place. —

—Gutsy.—

—And you aren't going to like this but the distributor is the same one as yours.

Jemma's stomach churned. After all these years of dealing with US Creameries, she felt betrayed.

—Are you okay? — Derek asked.

—Not really. Start looking for a new creamery closer to the Island. Blame the switch to shipping costs.—

—Will do. —

—When we find a new creamery, the old one will go. —

—OK—

—Shop cleanup going OK? —

—I hired a cleaning crew. Spanking clean. We are ready to open again early tomorrow as though nothing

happened. —

—You stepped up. Thx. —

—OK. Get back to Leo. —

Jemma turned to Leo. "Sorry. Last minute business."

"Everything okay?"

"Everything is perfect."

"Come here." He drew a line around each breast with his index finger. "I dream of tasting these."

His words sent shivers through her body like a magnetic field. She felt him work his warm hands to her backside and pull at her snaps. And then the release of the binder, setting her breasts free; they poured out. Leo received them with great pleasure as he buried his face in them, kissing, nuzzling, breathing them in. "That's what waffle cones will do to you," Jemma panned, not able to resist a joke at such a moment of desire.

Leo rolled to his side and burst out laughing. "Okay, babe."

There's that name again. It sounded better coming from Leo than Derek. She snuggled into him, noting his scent fresh air and salt water.

"Let's get rolling back to civilization." He slowly moved her aside, got to his feet, and held out his hand out.

Blushing with humiliation, Jemma refused his help and stood on her own. Why was Leo playing with her emotions? How could he start something and then end it on such a quick note? It was as though he didn't really care about her. It seemed a game to him. He feigned interest only to run from the situation once he set fire to it. A game. Obviously, she held no interest for him. That's when the wall around her heart began to build.

After returning all the used paper plates, and cups back into the bags, they left the food for small animals to finish. All the while, Jemma gathered her thoughts. A plan was coming together.

Jemma followed Leo once again, only this time, she was scooping her boobs back into the bra before snapping them in. On their way back to the car, she sent Larisa her first letter by email from her cell. It was only a few lines long and included a picture of Leo driving his sports car. Her beside him. Both with goofy grins on their faces. She typed: Is there a way to find a face recognition program to know the true identity of this person?

"Who are you sending that to?" Leo happily asked.

"Oh. A close friend who lives away from the island."

"I hope I get to meet her someday. I want to know all your friends." He squeezed her hand."

Chapter 11

The shop activity was busy, but her romance life slowed. It had been nearly a week since she saw or heard a thing from Leo. It was tempting to make some excuse to go to his cottage and check on him, but she didn't want to appear needy. Even if she carried an ice cream cake for him to try, he'd taste her desperation in it. So, she pushed away that idea and stuffed her feelings, this time with a healthy salad of romaine and garden vegetables. It was nighttime, and Jemma was nearly in bed when she heard email arrive. She dashed down the carpeted steps, into the kitchen, and sat in front of the lighted screen, checking her account. Along with lots of junk mail, there was correspondence from Larisa. Her feet did a happy dance as she clicked on the virtual envelope.

Dear Jemma,

Look at you! You sent an email! It's so much quicker. You will never go back to those pink envelopes again, although I loved them.

I did a bit of investigation myself for you. It was a face recognition algorithm of this man, and his name came up as Leo Stadler. I do believe you may have found yourself a winner in Leo. If anyone is deserving of love, it's you. You two look so happy jetting along the coast of your island. I love hearing from my readers, especially when they find love. You never gave up hope and

*received your happy ending. My work here is done. Yo
asked me several questions in one of your latest letter
but it's late. I must go. Get rest. Remain happy. If yo
never hear again from me as Larisa Stewart, just know
have so enjoyed our conversations.*

Love, Larisa

The email was cryptic and reeked of the possibilit
that Larisa would no longer correspond with her. Bu
why not? Jemma always looked forward to her advice
The week's events, starting with the broken mirror, ther
the brush off at the picnic, and lastly the email with the
tone of farewell from Larisa, left her with a weird
feeling. Was it the feeling of depression? For a year, the
author and the ice cream girl had a bond, but after finding
Leo, perhaps Larisa thought her work was done and Leo
could take it from here? But would he? And who was he
really? And in that moment, Jemma felt stronger. She'd
find a way out of any situation and never have to depend
on her ancestors, or Leo, or anyone. Everything she
needed was within her, including a way to make the shop
belong to her.

Later that night Jemma struggled to compose her
thoughts about Leo, and Harold, and Leo, and Derek, and
Leo, and Larisa, and Leo again, as she lay in bed
twisting and turning. It was then she became aware o
something that was in her room.

"So, you think you have it all figured out, little girl.
The voice creeped along her skin.

The night was heavy with humidity and the song
cicadas. Jemma turned in bed and pulled the covers ov
her head. She didn't want to talk with anyone. Least
all Harold. Maybe if she ignored the visit, they'd all

away and leave her to her plan. Yet, Tilly seemed unusually fretful, which was cause for alarm. Normally, she didn't seem to take notice. This time she whined and pawed at the blankets. Jemma also felt this visit was different. Like a soured vat of ice cream, it needed to be dealt with.

Jemma patted the pup, then sat up to focus her eyes in the moonless dark. The room was misty. Felt dampish. Far away, music played. A form stood in the far corner. It was still. Watching her. It was as if she was a spider caught in a web about to be eaten. Never had she ever felt in jeopardy with the visitations. The hair along her arms pricked. Once she wished for someone new to visit. Maybe she could renege on that wish. She glanced around the room. He was unaccompanied. She was alone with this specter. Was it the one she had been warned about?

"Eli?" Jemma shook. "Eli, is it you?"

"You know my name?" The voice lingered in the air as an echo.

"Harold mentioned you during his last visit."

"Yes, it's me. I'm the last resort in a prickly situation." Now the voice came in waves.

Jemma tried to relax as she looked again across the room. "Where is everyone?"

"I told them to stay home. Said I could handle this situation on my own."

"I imagine there's a lot to keep you busy when you're dead," she gingerly joked, thinking a funny line might lighten the situation. "Maybe another day and time would be best. I don't want to take up your time. Let's make an appointment."

"There's much you don't know, but that isn't why

I've come." Eli stepped from the darkness and became center stage, lit by a ghostly spotlight.

Jemma crossed her arms over her chest. "Wow, that's dramatic. Okay, I'm listening."

"You want lover boy. But what does he do? Don't you think it rather odd that he showed up at the same time as the chain ice cream shop did? Leo is using you, girl."

"This is a well-worn conversation. You picked up the discussion from where Harold left off. If you have something new to say, then say it. Otherwise, I am rather tired of this banter." Why was she was defending Leo after being rebuffed?

Eli walked the room, as another orb floated outside her window. This one was rather unusual and in the color of red. It reminded her of passion and wondered who it was.

"What does Leo do for a living?"

"He's a contractor." She mumbled the same vague answer Leo gave.

"Where's he from?"

"Mainland."

"Big place. Where is he staying on the island?"

"Blue cottage."

"See? You know nothing. Leo could be anyone. Probably a shyster. You need to realize that it's not the shop we are interested in; we are worried about you. You are the first female Singleton to run our operation and need protection. Guidance."

"I'm a female, but I'm just as smart as any of you male Singletons. And besides, as far as Leo is concerned, it's a private matter. I'm just getting to know him. Information about real estate takes time."

"Unfortunately, time is not on your side. We have been waiting for you to be proactive and get more information, so you know your next step."

"We recently found out that a big business is in the process of buying the place. But I have a plan to thwart that."

"That's our Singleton. Tell me. The others want to know upon my return."

"I'm a good saver. I met with a financial advisor. There is enough in my bank account to make an offer. I can snatch that shop out from under the big business." Jemma smiled, pleased with herself. "I can show you my bank statement. It's online. If you follow me down the steps to the computer, I'll show you. Or do you want to come in through the front door? Not really aware of how you all move about in a house, like are there rules or anything?"

"Pshaw. Listen to yourself. You said, 'big business.' My dear, they have so much more money than you, the little ice cream maker."

For the third time in a single week, Jemma felt deflated. "You are right. But don't count me out yet. I will figure this out without anyone's help."

"That's the Singleton attitude I've been waiting to hear. I believe in you."

"Gee, thanks." Jemma's spirits immediately lifted.

A loud horn blasted outside her window. Tilly barked as Jemma clapped her hands over her ears. "Ouch! What's that noise?"

"Band practice is starting. Must leave. You can do this, Jemma. Have faith in yourself. If you need another pep talk, just call."

"Wait, Eli. I have questions."

"Another time." Eli walked to the window and then jumped out of the second story.

Jemma woke late from a deep sleep. Gradually the memory of Eli's visit surfaced. Tilly seemed lackluster, wanting to stay in bed, which was opposite of how she usually acted, filled with energy.

When Jemma sat up, the covers dropped from her shoulders. After every previous visit, she had been so tucked into bed that it took work to untuck herself. Not this time. Eli? A new player in the family? Or was last night really a dream? With so much on her mind between all the new ghost faces and their comings and goings, along with the mess in her shop, and meeting Leo the love of her life, finding time for gleaning information, perhaps everything was colliding subconsciously as she slept, thus creating nightmares.

Needing to have a look at the wall pictures, Jemma dressed and hurried to the shop.

Derek was already serving coffee and scooping ice cream. Other than him being on time every day this week, everything else seemed normal. In fact, better than normal. She stood in front of the wall of pictures and noted they all were perfectly straight.

"Derek, was anything amiss when you arrived today?" Jemma asked casually in between customers.

"Amiss?"

"Nothing broken. Nothing crooked?"

"No. Why are you asking?"

"Nothing. Just checking. Hopefully, things will be a bit more normal going forward, but let me know if anything changes, okay?"

"Of course."

"In the meantime, I need to send out flyers and

emails to every shop and resident of the island," Jemma stated gingerly, hoping she could successfully pull off her plan.

"What do you have in mind?"

"Check your email in about an hour."

Jemma sat at her business computer in the office, and began her campaign.

Dear Islanders,

Since the conception of this town, we, the generational islanders, have owned and run Mermaid Island the way we see fit. Let's not allow an outsider to come and change all of that for us. If one shop goes, slowly, one by one, we will all be bought out. The time to act is now. Let's close ranks. If you live on the lower coast, please come to my shop and sign a petition to ban the sale of property to anyone who doesn't live year-round on this island. If you live inland or on the cliffs, I will bring a petition to you. Later today, I will be on the town square and hope to see you there. Together we can keep Mermaid Island the place we all want to live in and pass along to other islanders, and future generations.

Love and Ownership to Us,
Jemma Singleton

Jemma pressed print and hundreds of copies flew out of the printer onto the floor. She planned to pass them out among the island residents. Short on time, she had to move fast. On her way out of the shop, she dropped a hundred petitions on the tables, and across the counter top, telling Derek, "I need to talk to you about Leo."

"Oh, yeah, I forgot. He was here when I opened this morning. Said he needed to talk to you about something."

"Great, did he say where he was going?"

"No." Derek picked up one of the papers and read. Gave her two thumbs up. "Long live Mermaid Island. Jemma, you are a gem."

"It's good to be on the same team with you, finally."

"Ditto."

She pawed through her purse until her hand landed on her phone. She hit the button for Leo's number. No answer. Straight to voice mail. She took five deep breaths and felt her heart beating wildly in her chest. Where had he disappeared to? "I'll be back later. Thanks for covering for me again."

Derek breathed in deeply. "I smell a raise in my near future."

Jemma walked down the boardwalk in her uniform and pink shoes, heading to the chain ice cream shop, muttering its name along her way, "Mermaid Island's Best Ice Cream Shop. Best Ice Cream." This time, she'd walk right inside and speak to the owner. Of course, she'd use her inside, polite voice to get information. She turned the knob and opened the door. No one at the counter. No customers either. The place was empty except for a few tables. What was going on? There should be tables filled with patrons and sounds from the register ringing up orders. The bustle was missing. In fact, everything was missing but the bare bones. The place was unlocked. And no one seemed to be at home. Could Derek be wrong? He seemed so sure the new people had taken over the shop. Or, did they move out?

Warily, Jemma tip toed around the counter and into the storage room. "Hello?"

"Hello?" There was a flush of a toilet and a young

woman emerged from the restroom. "Oh, Jemma Singleton, it's you. You gave me a start. Didn't hear you come in."

"Yep, it's me." Jemma knew Anne Lily from the days when she babysat her. The thirty-something bleached blonde gal was owner of the island realty company.

"Just when we thought the place was sold, surprise, we are still waiting on the money wire. I'm wondering if it will even come."

"I heard the business was up and running."

"They started moving in a few days ago. I put a stop to it. No money. No contract equals no deal. They assured me the money would be here soon, but as I said, I need it in my hand with a signed contract first."

"Doesn't sound as though they are a company this island needs."

"Certainly not. I'm here checking on everything, and if I don't hear from them by end of day, the place will be up for sale again. So, you want to snoop around a bit?" Anne cheerfully offered.

"I certainly would." Jemma peered about without taking a farther step. "By the way, who is the buyer?"

"It's a blind sale. All I know is that the corporate office is in New York City. It has a front name of Buyers Industry, but beyond that, no individual's name. But they certainly have the money. All cash. Over asking price too."

"How much over asking?" Jemma worried she might be able to compete.

"One dollar. Can you believe it? I saw their finances. They can afford doubling the sale price."

"Then the building might be up for sale again?"

Jemma reiterated just to be sure.

"Yes, that's what I'm saying. It must come in by midnight. I'm sure this place will be gone quickly if this sale falls through. It's a hot market," Anne sweetly answered.

"So, a non-islander is buying the place?" Jemma felt hot.

"It seems as though you are judging me, Jemma. Business is business. The residents here have money but not like this. We don't have to wait for credit approval, or wait for them to secure a loan. It's perfect for me."

"But not for the island."

Anne bristled.

"May I have a look around while you're still here?" Jemma asked.

"Of course. Thinking of moving from your little space? I can get top dollar for your gem of a shop, it's the island's treasure."

"No, I'll never sell. But I am just curious to see this shop. I've never been in it since it was a tea shop."

"Have a look around. If all works out maybe you could expand your shop. Become a chain yourself. No hard feelings." She laughed and touched Jemma's arm for emphasis.

"Maybe a joint venture," Jemma supposed as she glanced about. "I won't be long."

"Take as long as you'd like. I'll wait outside."

The kitchen through the back of the dwelling was large, with wide counters for laying out trays of food or stirring up new recipes. There was also a huge walk-in pantry. A dozen shelves, cabinets galore, and wonderful restaurant type equipment. She didn't need all of that but some she sure could use. The store space itself was small, but that would be conducive to her fresh idea as well. The real gem was at the back of the store for her recipes. The front would be used for small focus groups by invitation only.

Jemma felt ready to present her offer and found Anne settled on a shaded bench. "I'd like to acquire this building. How can we make that happen?"

"First, I'd love to hear your plans." She patted the empty seat next to her.

"Long ago, I envisioned owning a development kitchen to create interesting dessert flavors. Get input from the public and by doing that, stirring excitement. Expand entirely from what I already am doing. This shop is it; my dream coming together. It can be a reality, if we can agree to terms."

"I don't think I can make that happen. A contract has to be signed."

"Anne, listen. I'm going to petition every shop owner, every resident on the island against you selling this property to anyone else but me."

"Jemma, dream on. It just can't happen." Anne patted her arm.

"Remember the time the Jenkinses wanted to buy the lovely house they are in right now?"

"That was before my time, but I am well aware." Anne glanced at her watch, seemingly impatient.

"At the time, they were non-islanders. But they had to sign a paper, promising to make that home their residence where they paid taxes in order to keep money here. Not off-island."

"I do recall. That was an interesting time. I wish I could do more. I have to sell to the first one who comes in with the money. I have a contract with another business. It's just a matter of time until it comes in. In fact, it might be at my office right now."

"What if I make the offer and am the first one to put down my money? Cash."

Anne's eyes widened. "You have that kind of cash? You don't need to apply for a loan?"

"My shop has done extremely well over the years. And I am a good saver. I pinch every penny that goes into the cash register."

"I'd do it. Yes, I would. But I can't. The money could be already wired to my office, so the sale would be theirs." Anne started to her feet.

"What if you don't go back to work today?" Jemma held on to Anne's purse and tugged Anne back to the bench.

"I simply can't do that." Anne shook her head.

"Anne, do you really want a non-islander to own a part of us? This shop is more than money. It's who we are. We live here year-round. A non-islander will only be interested in summers' profits. Then dash back to New York or wherever each winter. It's what the tourists do. And though the tourists are our lifeline to our lifestyle here, they aren't very nice people to deal with. Do we want more of that? Anne, we aren't all about profit either. We, you and I, and the shopkeepers, the residents, the one small school, the library, the one-man police department, the two-man fire station, we all are the heart and soul of what our ancestors have created and left for us. Doesn't that mean anything?"

Anne sighed and sat as though thinking it over. "You know, there is a lot of cleaning I need to do at home. Laundry too."

Jemma released her purse. Her voice cracked with

gratefulness. "Anne. Thank you."

"Nothing to thank me for. It's been a slow day, and I can't spend it waiting at the office for a call or a money wire. I might not be able to get back to the office till about seven or eight tonight. Listen, if you can get all the signatures you say that you can, and the asking price in cash, I can legally sell it to you."

Jemma eyes welled with tears and flowed down her face. "You will do that for me?"

Anne pulled one of the petitions from her hand. "Let my signature be the first. Give me a handful of these to take around to all the boardwalk shops. I will do that much for you. But there are other shops along the square, and I won't go to those. There's my license to protect if a complaint is lodged. Jemma, think. Your task is daunting. There are miles of coastline with remote cottages, hard to reach. I don't see how this can be done."

"You will do that much for me?" Jemma wiped tears. Even if this plan failed, she knew her dream would survive somewhere on the island. She hoped it was right here in the little shop.

"Yes, I am willing to go this far for you. Keep in mind, it's against my self-interest."

"Not in the long run." Jemma shifted on the bench. Her hands went numb with excitement, and she shook away their tingling. "Do I need to sign something?"

Anne dug into her briefcase. "I have an extra contract here. I will handwrite in your offer and make it void at 7:01 this evening. You have that long."

"Deal. I will offer two dollars above the asking price."

Anne quickly drew up the contract. "I filled in just enough to make it legal. Whoever gives me this amount first will own the shop." Anne stood. "I have a very dirty house to clean. And you better get going."

Chapter 12

Driving home, Jemma tried to reach Leo for the fifth time that day, but he still wasn't picking up. Just as well. This was a moment that only could be shared in person, if she could find him. Toe to toe. Face to face. Eye to eye. Jemma played the scene aloud. "My darling Leo, something wonderful has happened. A miracle. I want you to know, even before I tell Larisa Stewart."

"Wait." Jemma tapped the brakes as she careened around a sharp corner above the sea. Suddenly she realized, there was no way Larisa could be mentioned for two good reasons. Reason number one: Leo didn't know about her. Reason number two: Larisa and she no longer corresponded. Reason number three, and totally unrelated: She and Leo didn't know one another long enough to refer to him as "Darling." "And now, back to my story. Here is news of my dream that may, or may not, come true at precisely 7:01 tonight."

Jemma tapped on the steering wheel thinking about Leo wrapping his arms around her. Pulling her tightly into him. She'd nuzzle into his neck. Ooops. Eyes, she needed to look him in the eyes and say, "I'm buying another shop on the boardwalk to be my test kitchen. I want to share my recipes and try them out with you."

Buying another store was a big deal. An expensive one. Leo always asked about her dreams and today, she was happy to share them with him. Now with the possibility of it actually happening, she burst with joy to tell him. Maybe recruit him to help her, since he seemed to be pretty jobless at the moment. A phone call about her new endeavors just wouldn't do. Neither would delivering her news while wearing her white uniform and pink shoes.

Standing in front on her closet, Jemma felt like Cinderella as she dressed for the ball. Only instead of birds sewing her up into a gown, she settled on jeans and a blue button-down shirt. In place of a glass slipper, she chose running shoes. Only first, she cha-cha-ed into two body shapers, one for the top and the other for the bottom. Very carefully she applied her makeup, which she first looked up on Wecube to be sure she didn't come out looking like a clown, then brushed her hair into soft red curls below her shoulders. Standing in front of a full-length mirror, she thought she looked pretty darn decent, and probably ten pounds trimmer, which was always a good look.

On her way back to the boardwalk, she pulled into every inland cottage and each house dotting the cliffs, no matter how long the drive took. No one turned her down. Enthusiastically, several banded together to divide the island into zones to help cover the area.

The four o'clock afternoon sun was lowering by the time an elated Jemma tapped on the cottage's red door, noting how nice the place looked with the fresh deep blue paint on the shingles and light green steps leading to the same color on the porch. The place was trimmed with white with flower boxes holding sweet potato vines and red roses. She wished she knew the exterior designer; she could use similar colors at her place. But never mind all that now, good news abounded.

Her tap went unanswered. Perhaps, he didn't hear. She knocked. Then pounded. Still no answer. Either he wasn't home, or he was in the shower. Or had he gone back to the mainland without saying goodbye? The thought made her upset. She tried the doorknob. It turned. She stepped onto the hardwood floor. The one room cottage was cute with a twin bed on one side next to a dresser. She pulled out each drawer and clothes were folded nice and neatly. Wherever he was, his clothes remained. He'd be back.

Next, she noticed a large worktable with what looked like a state-of-the-art computer system on the other side. Books piled one on top of the other from floor to windowsill throughout the place. A leather couch and wooden table and chairs finished the decor along with a corner kitchenette and whitewashed walls. Jemma peered into the bathroom. Toilet, sink, towel, shower. No Leo. Again, she wondered why she hadn't seen him in so long.

Jenna seated herself on the couch for a moment, thinking how she'd tell Leo her news. It was her turn to take him for dinner. Or should she make him dinner at her place? It'd be the first time to entertain a date at her place. Her life was undergoing changes. Very positive changes. That is, if Leo would ever succumb to her wily advances. Perhaps along with her petition, she'd try to win his heart.

Minutes passed. Jenna stood eyeing the room, then walked around the space. Something disconcerting caught her eye. A pink envelope lay on the desk. The familiar lacy scroll of her writing was on the front, addressed to Larisa Stewart at the publishing house in New York City. Jemma moved closer and snatched it up.

The green computer light blinked, so she accidentally on purpose pressed the space bar. The screen flashed and there was the latest letter typed to her, from Larisa herself.

Dear Jemma,
Look at you! You sent your very first email...

At first Jemma was totally confused by this finding. Then she jerked out the side drawer to find a year's worth of her confidential letters she handwrote to her favorite romance author in all the world. How did Leo get a hold of these? Did Larisa Stewart ever receive a single letter to her? Could it be that all the correspondence she received was actually from Leo? What would make him, or anyone, do such a thing? Who was this cretin anyway? Why did he target her? What did he want of her? A wave of nausea washed over Jemma. Quickly she sat with her head between her legs, trying not to vomit.

A new ice cream flavor title whizzed through her mind, The Secret Life of Leo Stadler, BEWARE. Once you know a secret, you can never unknow it. Her private life no longer belonged to her. Her body flooded with embarrassment and shame. Would Leo tell the island people about her naivete? What was he planning to do with her?

Fury bubbled. How dare he toy with her affections to make a mockery of her. Or was he a hacker? Was she about to be blackmailed? Did he want to take over her business? Jemma scrunched the stack of pink envelopes that were akin to a running diary of her thoughts, dreams, and hopes—her letters.

"Jemma, are you sick? Are you all right?" He stood in the doorway, observing her collapsed in the arm chair before hurrying to her side. "Jemma, you look awful.

How can I help?"

"Where have you been?" It was then she noticed Leo with a duffel bag.

"I have been on the mainland, taking care of business." He set the bag down.

"What kind of business?" She held up the pink envelopes. "Does it have anything to do with these?"

"What? Did you go through my stuff? What do you think you are doing?" He tried to grab them, but she pushed him away. Tears streamed as Jemma walked around him heading to the door.

"You are snooping in my space." Leo glowered. "And now you are afraid of me?"

"What are you doing with these?" She kept a tight grip on the envelopes as she moved closer to the open door. "I think you are a dangerous man. You're stalking me. What were your plans?"

"Plans? You actually think I would hurt you?" He stepped toward her.

"Stay where you are, or I'll scream." Jemma warned, backing away. "You stole all my letters. Then you wrote to me under false pretenses. Even came to this island to meet me. You used me. For what? I'm just a middle-aged, single gal living on an island and selling ice cream. Very delicious ice cream, I might add. Tell me."

"Jemma, let me explain." He reached for her, but she sidestepped.

"Do you realize you also have committed a United States federal crime by removing my personal mail from my mailbox and can get into a lot of trouble for mail fraud? I'm sure there might be other serious crimes involved, but I can't think of them right now." She burst into tears. She hugged the letters tightly against her body, not wanting to drop one of them. The words and the emotions she wrote about were only fodder for some sick male ego. Realizing her love for Leo was misguided, finally realizing he didn't care about her. There would be no winning anyone's heart. Only lots of pain to work through.

"I didn't intercept your letters. Look. They all have the post office stamp." He walked to her, then pried open her arms to jerk out one of the envelopes. Smoothing it out, he held it up for her to see.

"Stand back, away from me," Jemma seethed.

"Okay." He backed away. "I hate that you are so afraid of me."

Jemma grabbed the envelope and studied the meter stamp, then she ratted through the rest, noting they all had the meter mark. She watched every muscle in his face go slack with concern. "They do have a postmark. Then how did you get them? Are you a New York mailman who steals mail? I've heard of that happening. You never have been clear about your career."

"My publisher sent them to me," Leo explained with a shrug.

"You have a publisher? Are you serious?" She rolled her eyes in frustration. "Now I've heard it all."

"You addressed the letters to Larisa Stewart, at my publisher's Manhattan address. They sent them to me here to read and to answer. It's protocol. Let's sit down, okay? I have something to tell you, but it's not what you think."

"I'll remain standing, thank you."

"You do deserve the truth, and it's just what I'll give you. It's going to be a bit shocking, and if you never want to see me again, I understand."

"I already never want to see you. First start with where you have been for the past week?"

"On the mainland. I already told you."

"Doing what?"

"Private business." He became angry. "I come home and catch you going through my things, and you have the nerve to ask me where I have been?"

"You disappeared without so much as a goodbye or phone call. I found these when I came here to tell you my news."

"What news?"

"Never mind that now. What are you doing with these letters? I want to know who you work for." She stared at him for a beat, then closed her eyes briefly and shook her head in exasperation.

"I'm a writer. I work for National Publishers."

"A writer? I do not believe you."

"It is still the truth."

Her eyelids fluttered and she looked at him in surprise. She tugged her phone from her pocket. "Tell me your name so I can look you up."

"You won't find the information you need on Google."

"Another deflection," she huffed. "Another lie?"

"Will the real Larisa Stewart sit down?" he asked, then sat. He held out his hand inviting her to sit beside him. "Nice to meet you."

"Cut the crap. I'm serious here, and you are full of shit."

"Please sit. Let me finish." Leo swallowed hard.

"So, you know Larisa Stewart. Are you two in this together? Is she your girlfriend?" Jemma held her ground.

"I write under a false name. An assumed name. A pseudonym. Women don't really like reading romance from a male author for some reason. The books wouldn't sell well under my name, so my agent and I came up with this idea, to publish under a woman's name."

Jemma sank back into the couch. It was hard to tell what was real anymore. Ghosts, ghost writer, pseudonyms, therapists, crooked pictures, romance writers. She wanted to believe Leo—he did look forlorn—but she hated to give in and be hurt. Crushed. At the moment, she felt she'd never be able to trust anyone ever again. It would take a huge leap of faith to welcome him back. "Why didn't you just tell me that in the first place? Right now, my head and my heart are at war with each other. I really want my heart to be right."

"Let me appeal to your heart. I'm under a strict no-disclosure contract. I live in Manhattan, raised in the Bronx. I have a younger brother and an older sister. My parents are divorced. Anything else? There are so many more things you don't know. I want you to know everything about me, down to every thought I have. I owe you the entire truth. But I've hurt you. I should've ignored your letters, or sent a formulaic letter in response as I do with everyone else, but I wanted to connect with you. I found you interesting. Smart. Then I met you, and you're incredibly funny and sexy. My favorite combination."

"Stop making me melt." She raised an eyebrow and smiled a bit. Hope itched her heart. Her lips tingled with desire for a kiss. As he moved closer, she watched her future unfold.

Leo took her hand. "I want to know you. I've wanted

to make love to you since that first day when you told me about your newest ice cream flavor. But, since you didn't know the real me, since I was here to meet you without full disclosure, I made myself pull back, and let me tell you, it wasn't easy."

"That explains so much." The time in the ice cream parlor, and again at the picnic when he suddenly withdrew. It was making sense. Darn, but she was beginning to believe him. That is, she wanted to believe him. Thank goodness this conversation was out of earshot of the pictures in her shop.

"The letters arrived to me through my publishing house. I wrote to you first in Manhattan, then from here, but mailed them from the mainland so you wouldn't find out about me," he further explained.

"Okay. I suppose you can prove this."

"Let me get my contract." Leo crossed the room to his desk and after a bit of rummaging, handed her the document.

She read it over and over again. "Looks official."

"What else can I do to prove that I'm an honest guy who is truly interested in you? I'd never do anything to hurt you."

"But you have hurt me. You lied to me. Why should I believe you now?" She wiped her tears using the bottom of his shirt.

"No more deceit. It was a big piece of theater. You're endearing and breaking my heart." Leo threaded his fingers through her hair.

"I want to believe you. It seems farfetched, but plausible."

"Give me a chance. Allow me to prove myself. Open disclosure."

"I need time."

"For the rest of my life, I pledge to hold the car door open for you. You'll come home to roses. I'll write love sticky notes to you and put them all around the house. I'll kiss you every day. Long ones. And date nights. Lots of date nights. We'll slow dance in the garden, and in the winter by the fireplace. I'll always adore you. You can count on me. I'll listen to you. Talk to you. Dream with you. I'll take you to New York for you to meet my publisher. He will vouch for me. I'll make reservations right now. First class." He pulled the cell from his back pocket.

"Stop. What makes you think I'd go anywhere with you?"

"I was hoping."

"Second chance? What makes you worthy of that?"

He thought for a moment. "I'm not worthy of a second chance."

"What other genres do you write under assumed fake names? Murders? Historical?" Her words were hard, but her tone by now had softened.

"No others. Just romance by your favorite author."

"Former favorite author." Jemma stared at Leo, thinking how much she already missed a woman that never existed. Right now, she could use buckets of advice from Larisa Stewart. But there was no Larisa Stewart. She had to figure this out for herself.

"I'm falling in love with you, Peaches."

Jemma brightened. "Of course, liars can say that too."

Leo looked around the room, then frantically opened his bank information on the screen. "Look. Here is my bank account. You can scroll through the last year and see all the deposits from book sales through my publisher."

Jemma studied the screen, trying to seem disinterested only to be impressed with the bank deposits. "Okay, you are starting to convince me. At least I know you aren't a serial killer."

They laughed.

"It feels good to laugh with you."

"But you still might be a stalker," Jemma teased.

"Not a stalker. You want me gone and I will leave the island."

"No. Don't leave. Stay."

Leo embraced her then kissed her forehead. "By the way, why were you here when I walked in?"

Jemma had quite forgotten her news until Leo reminded. "I bought something today."

"Tell me." He held her at arm's length and looked into her eyes.

"Guess." Jemma felt her flirty side kick into full gear.

"A new car?"

"Bigger."

"Ah. You are riddling with me. I can tell that forgiveness is right around the corner." He smiled.

"Don't be so cocky. Forgiveness takes time. In the meantime, I will give a clue. It's old."

"Bigger than a car and old. A boat? Airplane? Hot air balloon?"

"I am in the process of buying Mermaid Island's Best Ice Cream Shoppe."

"How did that happen?"

"It's a long story, but I need to get to the island square with all my petitions as soon as possible."

"Let me help. I'll come with you."

"You're not an islander. Why do you want to help?"

"Because you're my girl."

"Your girl. If only I could believe that. Where is my guarantee that you won't break my heart?"

Leo gently moved her to the side. "Sit." He pointed to the couch, then rolled his chair up to the screen. In a minute he was quickly keyboarding. In ten minutes, he hit print and handed her fifteen pages.

"Anyone can say anything. I need action."

"Just shut up and read," he insisted.

Jemma leaned back on the couch as Leo brought her iced tea and sugar cookies. He sat across the room from her and studied her face as she read. Once in a while she'd look up and murmur, "Stop doing that. That is an order."

The story was about a man who lived on an island called Manhattan. In the midst of millions of people, he found himself alone, day after day and night after night. All the manuscripts he wrote, never sold. One day, he invented a new name and wrote romance stories of things he imagined for himself. Then one day, a bird flew into his window holding a pink envelope. He looked at the scrolly writing and thought, this person must be an artist to form these letters so perfectly. Then one day, in his loneliness, he decided to find this rare gem of a person. The moment he saw her, he thought she was more beautiful and funnier than he could have ever imagined or write on a page. Her essence was light and airy, and beyond compare. In that moment he decided he would try to win her heart, but she couldn't know his true identity because he couldn't reveal his name, and knew she'd feel betrayed once she discovered it. But once she learned that he loved her, she would forgive him for then she'd realize the depth of his commitment, and that they were destined to be together. From that moment on, he pledged his heart and life to her. And then he waited quietly to find out her answer. Will she forgive him and be with him?

Jemma finished reading all the pages, which were double spaced and in the correct margins. Everything was perfectly spelled, and the grammar was excellent. The story melted her heart, but she wouldn't give in so easily. She stood to her feet, crossed the room, and handed them back. "Maybe. Let me think on it. My heart is very involved with you. This is the most preposterous story I ever have heard, but it could possibly be true. It is just that I am having a hard time letting go of my doubt. However, I am willing to give you another chance. Leo, let's take it slow and see what happens. I need trust and complete honesty before we can go further in this relationship." She held her breath, then released slowly.

"Whatever makes you feel most comfortable. I'm willing to spend time to build trust back between us. You are worth all the trouble you cause." He chuckled as he kissed the back of her hand. "I want to repair what I never meant to break."

"I need to get to the square. Come with me, famous writer?" Jemma held out her hand.

Walking out the door into the sunlight, nothing had changed but the traffic. There was none. Puzzled, Leo led Jemma onto the boardwalk. Only a few frustrated tourists remained pulling on locked shop doors.

"What time is it?" Jemma twisted Leo's watch about to see. "It's after six. We've got to get to the square."

"But where is everyone?"

"Hopefully they are there. Come on," Jemma called, getting into her car.

Driving slowly down the streets, they were amazed to see the crowds of people gathering near the historical courthouse. "This island used to be its own county before it was annexed. Ever since, people are keenly aware of not wanting to lose their independence to the mainland in order to live by their laws and rules."

"That explains a lot. I take it this is about your petition?" Leo surmised.

"Yes, let's hope it's for my good and not an anti-Jemma protest."

Not able to find a parking spot, they parked in the middle of the street and walked hand in hand up the courthouse steps where Anne stood holding petitions and her contract. Applause went up as the numbers of people saw Jemma, who suddenly felt weak in the knees.

Anne held a bullhorn. "As you can clearly see, the people of Mermaid Island agree that the ownership of any part of its soil belongs with these people and generations to come. Due to these petitions, all the residents will petition that only the people who are all-year residents can also be property owners."

"Meaning, no one can own property on the island unless they live here year-round?"

"Exactly. It will only make our property more and more valuable in time. Commitment. Now, for the next piece of business; Jemma it's nearing the eleventh hour. I need from you a cashier's check plus one dollar to purchase said property."

"Oh no. I didn't get to the bank. Will you take a personal check?" Jemma meekly asked.

"I can, but do need a down payment in cash right now. Then you can sign the papers for transfer of deed."

"I don't have that kind of cash on me. Who would? You never mentioned it earlier or I'd have it ready."

Fern stepped forward. "Jemma, over the years, you have given me produce and by doing so saved my ass, many a day. I'll open my safe at the restaurant and give you what I have."

"I'll pay you back in the morning, I promise."

"No hurry to pay me back. Take your time," Fern said as he headed toward the boardwalk.

"Well, you better hurry, Fern," Anne yelled after him. "The contract is only in play till seven oh one. That's fifteen minutes."

Andy stepped out from the crowd. "If Fern doesn't have enough, I'll sell my boat to Leo who was asking about it this morning. That is if he has cash?"

"Yes, I haven't had a chance to get to the bank to deposit this cashier's check sent from my publisher. I'll sign it over to you, Anne."

"That'll work," Anne said.

"Andy, I know how much you love that boat. I'll sell it back to you in the morning," Leo said.

Noah took the bullhorn. "This idea is brilliant. Only islanders can buy on this island. It starts right here and now with Jemma purchasing the shop. I'm asking someone to take off their hat to pass around for a collection. I aim we get way more than is needed to validate the contract and keep Jemma and a historic gem right here with us."

Pat Jenkins stepped forward. "I can help too. I'll temporarily sign over my house to the real estate office for the remaining amount. I knew our Jemma was in trouble, so I brought my house title with me. Will that work, Anne?"

"Yes, that'll work."

"Pat, I can't let you do this." Jemma grabbed his arm.

"For many years, Miss Jemma, you have served my wife and myself with joy and happiness. The ice cream was good too, but we really came to see you. You sing and dance your desserts over to us. When your parents died, you took on the mantle of a historical shop with gusto. It's the least I can do. Especially with Beth declining so much recently, I want her last true thoughts to be helping you out."

"It's seven now, people," Anne nervously announced.

"I'm back," Fern declared racing up the steps to hand Anne a wad of money. "Hope it's enough."

"It's enough." Anne nodded.

Jemma thought she was about to be hugged to death with all the good wishes she suddenly received by the crush of the crowd.

As the evening wore on, more and more left the square to head home. Leo and Jemma walked to her new shop and carried the old sign to the beach where Leo lit in on fire. They sat on a log to watch it burn.

"Are we okay?" Leo wanted to know.

"We are more than okay." Jemma snuggled into his side.

"I think we are okay too. And you owe a lot of people money in the morning. So glad I'm not you." Leo laughed. "Let's go back to my place and have a celebration drink."

Jemma loved how cozy the blue cottage seemed

tonight. She watched Leo pour two drinks. She held her glass high to toast. "Here's to us. And no more secrets."

"No more secrets."

"There's something I need to tell you too, Leo."

"I'm listening."

Jemma took a deep breath and squeezed Leo's hand tightly. "It's my turn to tell you an improbable story. But first, do you believe in ghosts?" Then she walked across the room and sat in his rolling chair to begin to keyboard her story.

Chapter 13

It was late evening of a new season. The tourists vacated the island, leaving behind boarded-up, un-winterized cabins, while fall settled in with icy ocean breezes. The Little Shoppe of Gourmet Dreams was open and brimming with flowers of congratulations along with good wishes from the boardwalk shop owners and the people of Mermaid Island.

Jemma smiled as she finished creating her newest recipe, combining cherries and cake with nuts and ice cream. Not only was she continuing with the success of her family's ice cream parlor with Derek as manager, but by inspiration and hard work, had created this new business of specialty desserts. At last, she had the space to create and hold venues to taste test unusual sweets. The first priority remained selling her ice cream recipes to creameries all over the country with Mermaid Island's logo. The profit from that, she turned back into supporting the arts and struggling businesses.

A cold breeze leaked through the old building around the windows. Bundled in a sweater, Jemma cleaned the kitchen, overwrought with excitement to spend the evening with Leo. She hand-dried the glass dishes and carefully stacked them on open shelves, while deciding which lingerie set to tantalize Leo. *Should it be the lacey lavender bra and panties?* She wondered. *Or the red see-through bra trimmed in black ribbon that also crisscrossed across the bodice?* She giggled over the memory of Leo referring to the ribbons as "cables." How could he ever mistake the delicacy of satin ribbon to a rope that moors ships? Jemma shook her head and giggled more.

A tap-tap-tap drew her toward the window. There was Leo, bundled against the cold with his coat collar pulled up. Jemma flung down the towel and dashed to the door, which she jerked open, before pulling him into the shop. Without a word, she threw her arms around him and planted wild kisses on his neck and face.

"Whoa, slow down. We have the entire evening to look forward to."

"There's no time like the present." She untied her apron and tossed it over her shoulder.

"How was your first day at your Taste Test Parlor?" he asked, opening her sweater and slowly unbuttoning her blouse.

"As you can see, lots of love being tossed my way." She pointed at the gifts, flowers, and notes of congratulations.

"Wow, impressive." Leo pulled away to take a closer look.

"How's Larisa Stewart's new series selling?" Jemma hugged him.

"Like hot cakes. I started the new series about you and Mermaid Island, and your ghostly visits. All fiction, of course." He turned around and winked, kissing her forehead.

"Of course, it's all fiction." She returned his wink. "So, you got the go-ahead from your publisher to do the new series?"

"I did and with enthusiasm. I'm writing that series

under my own name, which is so liberating." He pulled out a folded paper from his coat pocket. "This is the prelim workup from the marketing department."

"'New author Leo Stadler has a distinguished style of storytelling that separates him from the rest. We see a place in the market for this type of fantasy. Let's greenlight for a trilogy. We can go from there,'" Jemma read. "I am so proud of you."

"Thanks."

"Can you handle two book series at once?"

"I can do anything." He twirled her around.

"Let me show you just how proud I am of you." Jemma pulled him by his suspenders and tugged him tightly into her. She parted his lips with her tongue and kissed him deeply. As he squeezed her rear, she became aware of his desire growing against her, which increased her desire. Her fingers released the paper from her fingertips, and it drifted to the floor.

"Hey, I hear there's a desk in an office back there," Leo softly whispered, looking over her shoulder.

"I do believe I saw one, but darn, it's full of papers. But there's also a long table with nothing on it."

Just then, Derek slung open the backdoor. "Hello, lovebirds!"

The couple whirled around.

"How was your first day as manager at The Little Shoppe of Ice Cream Delights?" Jemma asked, releasing Leo from her grip.

"Great. Packed house. The two new hires should work out fine. And I'm thinking about asking one of them out." He cockily rocked back on his heels.

"Not a good idea. Keep business, business. No playtime. If you want to date someone, do not hire them.

A lot of bad stuff can come from that and put the business in jeopardy." Jemma waved her finger in the air.

"That's what I've been very recently told."

"I have the feeling there is something you aren't telling me," Jemma said.

"Since you opened this new business in this building, have you had any special visitors?"

"Special visitors like?"

"Your family?"

"Ah. No. Not a single visit. So, tell me, you've already had a visit. Was it about being flirtatious with the employees?"

"Yes. And it wasn't pleasant."

Jemma and Leo laughed.

"Why do you think you haven't had any visits?" Derek asked.

"Probably because this place is all mine. No skin in this game. But I do think, if I needed them, they'd come. That's just what they do."

"Tell me about your visit, Derek." Leo pulled his cell out to record.

"It was last night. I was asleep, alone in bed, and there was a terrible noise pounding on the window. Outside I saw balls of light. I felt compelled to open the window when they flew right into the room. After some bouncing around the room, a bubble burst, or something like that, and there was Harold with Eli. They argued with each other and bossed me."

"I've experienced that as well. What was the nature of this visit?"

"Basically, not to date employees."

"Anything unusual at the shop this morning?"

"Crooked pictures."

"They can be difficult, but remember they care about you, even if it seems they don't."

"I had three hours of sleep last night."

"Sorry. Did you wake up all tucked in tight?"

"How did you know?"

"Lucky guess." She cackled.

"Oh, this morning, the Jenkinses came in as usual. I named their table Let's Fall in Love Again."

"Kind of a long name. Did they like it?" Jemma gathered her belongings.

"Loved it. I see you two are ready to head home. I guess I'll be going, too. Oh, I nearly forgot. I also met Vera."

"Ah. My great-aunt, beware. She scolded me about the button-popping incident."

"I do recall that. It was the day Leo first came into the shop." Derek nodded at him.

"When our love began." Jemma teasingly gushed. "She's dignified and a bit uppity. Maybe proper is a better word choice. Be careful how you dress. If you are sloppy or have a stain on your shirt or apron, she will have a word with you. Also, if you are short with a customer, you better believe she will note it. Other than that, you will enjoy working with her."

"Working with her?" Derek groaned.

Jemma gritted her teeth. "You have inherited them all now."

"Geez." Derek rolled his eyes. "By the way, she said she left something for you. Didn't tell me what."

"That's odd. I wonder what it was."

"I'm sure there will be no doubt when you find it," Derek said.

Jemma smiled, remembering her strictness. "Well,

try to get some rest tonight."

"I'm following Derek out and stopping on the way home for fresh lobster and a bottle of wine. I can't wait. I'll see you at home, Peaches." Leo turned off the recorder.

"You will, but before you leave, I need another kiss." She wrapped her arms around him and kissed him hard. Then watched as he got into his car and drove away. About to walk out, her foot struck something on the floor. A small blue and red tin object spun about before hitting the wall. She picked up the toy whistle and warmly smiled. "Vera. Are you wishing me well? Or Latimer, are you up to some tricks?"

Jemma shut the door and stopped to admire the recent paint job of Copen Blue trimmed in Agreeable Gray siding with a Sequin colored door. As she turned toward the parking lot, she heard a whistle. She cocked her head to listen again. It was a distinct toy whistle. Quickly checking her purse, she found the whistle where she just placed it, still tucked neatly into the side pocket. Jemma looked around, then stared down the boardwalk. "One more stop, Leo," she whispered.

Jemma stood inside the shop her great-great-great-grandfather started more than a century earlier, staring again into the many faces in the pictures. "Go easy on Derek. He's kind of fragile. You scared the b'jeebers out of him with your visit. Give him space to grow. I promise to keep an eye on him as you did me. If there's a problem I cannot handle, you will be the first ones I'll call, after Leo, that is. By the way, you might want to give Leo another chance. He's a good guy. In the meantime, I'm going to miss this place and everyone single one of you. Especially you." She tapped the glass over Harold's face.

Then, taking her time, she looked into each face as she stepped from frame to frame to frame.

The room lights flickered, then dimmed. "Don't tell me the electric wiring is bad." Jemma worried to herself as she played with the light switch. As if filling a balloon, the atmosphere grew to an eerie shade of dusk, making Jemma mechanically back away from the wall in time to see her dead ancestors emerge, making their frames wildly swing from nails, scraping the wall behind.

Her eyes filled with light as the dozens of orbs drifted along the ceiling like lanterns. They melted and dripped in the colors and flavors she created. Perhaps guided by family, transparent festive streamers appeared, then whirled about. Fascinated, in a trance-like state, Jemma moved along with them. It occurred to her that she was part of a plan. It was more than simply inheriting a coastal shop. She had been cared for and guided by generations of family who loved her.

The drips from the ceiling faded, as did the streamers. Jemma stood still as the orbs took on their human form. They joined hands as they circled about her, rotating, smiling, silently wishing her well. Present were the spirits she knew from nighttime visitations, along with the spirits who had never visited but she'd wondered about. "I'm so glad you came. For years, I looked into your faces and wondered about you. Here we all are together, finally."

In a moment's time, the new spirits conveyed their stories. Jemma took it all in quickly. At last, one by one they said their goodbyes, then returned to the pictures on the wall. Harold and Eli were nearly the last. It was nice to see the brothers getting along. Ralph wiped a tear as he bounced away. Her aunts giggled as they tossed air kisses in her direction. Latimer threw a chocolate ice cream cone at her, then ran across the room. He was the final spirit to hop back into his picture.

As she turned off the light and opened the door, she turned once again to say,

"Remember, you are always mine. I am always yours."

A word about the author...

As an educator, I can't seem to stop teaching. I have two amazing adult children and two adventuresome grandsons. When not writing, I garden as though my life depends on it. My tidy residence is near Dallas, Texas.

Interesting fact: It's not unusual for my book characters to wake me during the night, brooding about their names or filled with plot twist suggestions. Occasionally, there's whining over what I've written about them (they are quite vain at times), pouting if they don't get enough book mention. They will even scheme together concerning the next chapter. Sometimes, a new villain emerges to all our surprise.